MANY PEOPLE DIE LIKE YOU

MANY PEOPLE DIE LIKE YOU

Lina Wolff

Translated from the Swedish
by Saskia Vogel

SHEFFIELD – LONDON – NEW YORK

First published in English in 2020 by And Other Stories
Sheffield – London – New York
www.andotherstories.org

'Nuestra Señora de Asuncion' first published in Swedish by *Granta*, 1, 2013 and in English by *Granta*, 124, 2013.

'Year of the Pig' first published as 'Grisens år' by Dagens Nyheter, 2017; previously unpublished in English.

All other stories in this collection were published as *Många människor dör som du* by Albert Bonniers Förlag, Stockholm.

9 8 7 6 5 4 3 2 1

ISBN: 9781911508809
eBook ISBN: 9781911508816

Editor: Anna Glendenning; Copy-editor: Ellie Robins; Proofreader: Sarah Terry; Typesetter: Tetragon, London; Typefaces: Linotype Neue Swift and Verlag; Cover design: Lotta Kühlhorn. Printed and bound by CPI Group (UK) Ltd, Croydon, CRO 4YY.

And Other Stories gratefully acknowledge that our work is supported using public funding by Arts Council England and that the cost of this translation was defrayed by a subsidy from the Swedish Arts Council and a grant from the Anglo-Swedish Literary Foundation.

SWEDISH
ARTSCOUNCIL

CONTENTS

It's not the first time I've seen a badly written report, but this one is worse than usual. Not that I have anything against dangling modifiers. I know how it is – to avoid a dangling modifier, one must be willing to sacrifice the flow. Perhaps he was not willing. But how am I to tell? You can't tell whether a man knows how to modify just by looking at his face.

And the adjectives! From the very first line, the way they're crammed in there is vulgar, and they go on to form a banal, soupy mess.

Language aside, the report is bizarre. It's full of images, intimate images, and it has none of the matter-of-fact, concise, and streamlined qualities I requested. Furthermore, the photographs are out of focus. So much so that in certain images the people in question are barely identifiable.

"Text," I'd specified when commissioning the assignment. "I want only text. Is that clear?"

"Yes," he'd replied.

I meet his gaze. He looks away, and there's no mistaking what underlies the writing of this report. Pity, and then something stronger than pity – the pleasure of presenting a certain kind of fact.

How perverse. As if I weren't paying him enough.

I go to the liquor cabinet and pour myself a glass. I sit on the couch and take him in. He is tall, corpulent. Bulky. He could be my type, if you looked past his dullness.

"I presume the report is incomplete without commentary."

"I have lots to say. May I sit?"

"Yes."

He sits down and says:

"I usually start off my case presentations with a brief account of the subject's life. Much of what I'm about to say will already be familiar to you, of course. But I'm telling you so you know what I know. So you know I crossed my t's and dotted my i's, so to speak."

"I understand."

"So, I shadowed your husband, Joan Roca Pujol. He works as an architect at an office in the center of Barcelona, Avenida Diagonal. At present, he's working on a project for the town of Sitges. His brief is to restructure the town center in response to the large influx of homosexual tourists with serious spending power. There will be increased space for local trade, and the urban planning will foreground the area's creative capital. Is this part of the report accurate?"

"Yes."

"Your husband is spending a lot of time in Madrid. Which, taking into account his professional situation, he shouldn't be. Your suspicion stems from these long stays in the capital. You suspect there's another reason. A woman."

"Or man."

"In that case, I can confirm that this is about a woman."

The corner of his mouth twitches, up and at an angle. It could be interpreted as a smile. I remember the fish I put in the oven just before he arrived. It should bake for exactly an hour, on gas mark seven. The table is already set; I set it right after lunch, as always. I was faithful to my habit. I am faithful. Loyal. I am loyal as a dog. A very dumb dog.

A woman, then. Hair color, teeth, chest size. What else? A city. Every person is a city, Joan says – occupational hazard. In his world, I'm like Verona. I'm like a balcony he can look up at, hoping some feeling might yet sprout inside him. Some he describes as Detroit, or Bonn. Perfect infrastructure but dull. Others are like Venice. The other woman may well be like Venice. As sticky as ice cream and hot. Stinking. Flaking facades. Yes, that's it. That's probably what she's like. Mold-flecked masks and rotting foundations.

Decadence that knocks you senseless.

I have a few minutes before the fish has to be taken out.

"Continue."

"Yes, a woman. Would you like to know her name?"

"No."

"Well, it's in the report. They meet every Thursday and Friday. Every other week, he spends the weekend at her place."

"I understand. Now give me the details."

He flips through the papers. Back and forth, looking at the pictures. Opening his mouth, closing it again. Theatrical. He shuts the report.

"May I speak from the heart?"

"Yes."

"Then I'll begin by saying – and I hope it will be of some comfort – that when they meet, your husband turns off the light as soon as he can. You see, her face frightens him."

"Frightens him?"

"Yellow teeth. Smoking and obscene living. Her skin is ruined."

"More details, please."

"Details hurt."

"My pain is none of your concern."

"What do you want to know?"

"Everything."

He says:

"The other woman – she lives in Madrid, by the way, on Calle Calvario – thinks mostly of her debts nowadays. Somehow, her apartment is full of them, and she thinks he, Joan, should toss her a few bills from time to time. Not large sums, but he does eat there and sometimes spends days in a row with her. Then there's his bad habit of taking long showers after their . . . well, after their lovemaking. He must use upwards of 300 liters sometimes, according to the woman's own calculations (which are probably incorrect – she isn't the sort of woman who's used to dealing with numbers, you get me?). But she has pointed out to him that she grew up wanting, so it's not like she doesn't know how to run a household, but there are all those wasted hours, time she could have spent doing other – profitable – activities. She's preparing this talk she wants to have with Joan carefully. Suggestions like these can be misunderstood."

"Is that so?"

"Yes, he could mistake her for . . . a prostitute."

"Say whore."

"Well then. Whore. If that's what you want."

I take a drink. The heat spreads – as it does with this kind of whiskey. It's like aftershave, but internal. I meet his gaze. Hold it. And he turns away. Of course, he wants a drink. He longs to have something in his hands, because this isn't exactly going as he'd hoped. My silences and my word choices trouble him and so he wants alcohol. But he must wait; I'll be the first to intoxication, that's my prerogative.

"May I see it?"

He hands me back the report. Beads of sweat have formed around his nose.

I flip through the pages.

"Is it typical of the detectives' guild to shoot out-of-focus images?"

"Typical of *the guild*? Do you have a lot of experience with detectives? Other than me?"

"One hears things."

"We have to keep a certain distance. We can't just walk over, stick the camera in their face, and tell them to say 'cheese.'"

"I understand."

"Then there's her skin. It takes a while before you see what's off about her face. But then you see it: a rough surface."

"Which he loves. Continue."

"The lines. There's something severe about them. She is not a beautiful woman."

"Which makes everything much worse. A surface can be erased. But not an interior."

He looks at his hands. Says:

"In any case, those lines around her mouth are sharp. She says it's unfair that you women must suffer time. You're so soft, after all. She says time should handle you more carefully. But that's not something that can be legislated, is it?"

He appears to be stifling a giggle.

I told you: he's bizarre, just like the report. But he gets going after that giggle, perhaps thinking he can talk it away, wash it down with word mush. Pointing, gesticulating. Drawing flattering comparisons between me and the other woman. That's what detectives do, what they've always done, in every book and throughout time. He's probably thinking it won't be long before I'm in tears. Then he'll take a starched handkerchief from his jacket pocket, wipe my nose, and say "there, there." And I'm supposed to put my head on his shoulder. Then the embrace, the cocoon of empathy, and his retainer for further assignments, leaving my account at the end of each month.

He gets up. Walks around the room. Stops by the shelf of family photos, and says:

"There are solutions."

"Solutions?"

"Yes. We know how to get rid of people."

Joan and I are smiling at each other in our wedding photo. Behind us is a wealth of happy people, and a bouquet of roses flying through a sky of white petals. I look out the window. You can see for miles today. It's a beautiful night, very clear.

"Would you like to eat? Dinner's ready."

"No, thank you. But I'd love something to drink."

"Gin? Vermouth?"

In a flash, I return with his drink.

"Let's go back to 'solutions.' How would that work exactly? Would I get photographic evidence?"

"Oh yes, we can arrange all of that. And you can choose the murder weapon."

"What a macabre term."

"Macabre acts require macabre terminology. It doesn't take much getting used to, and then it really is enjoyable. I have other examples – "

"That's not necessary. I'm not interested."

"Aren't you?"

"Not at all."

"So why the questions?"

"Female jealousy. Wouldn't that justify exploring a hypothetical extermination?"

I laugh, and the laugh seems to echo. He is serious, sitting with his glass in hand. He's not an ugly man. Not beautiful, not ugly. Perfectly average.

"You're being glib," he says. "As if you don't understand how serious I am. If you want we can continue. Otherwise we drop it right now. When it comes to revenge, you have to make a choice. You can't stay in no man's land."

No man's land. The drink goes to my head, and this is precisely what I'd like to discuss. The no man's land. I have an exceptional tolerance for the no man's land. Drip a drop of that on the threshold and you'll see how it expands, spreading through the room and the entire marital abode, and finally entering me. Then it continues out into the city and disappears. Soon it's gone, vaporized.

"Aha."

He squirms. Says:

"She's just a simple whore."

"I'm sorry?"

"Or slut, because she doesn't even know to get paid for it."

"Do you think insulting her will get you a bigger tip?"

"Now you're the one insulting me. But I suppose that's how it goes: the insulted insult. The darkness has to go somewhere."

*

I go to the kitchen. Take the fish out and light the candles on the table. I hear his voice. It sounds happy, surprised, excited.

"A phallus!"

He's walked into the office and is at the drafting table.

"What a fantastic drawing! Is it yours?"

"No, it's Joan's."

"Aha, I've watched him work, but you never see the finished product through the window."

"It's the best thing that's been drawn on Sitges' dime to date."

There's something about that picture. It makes everyone who sees it happy, exactly as it's supposed to. I'm no exception.

"It's a proposal for a fountain, did you know that?"

No, he did not, and I tell him. The idea: stiff and straight, water spraying from its tip. A towering urban orgasm, you could say, to take place day and night, thirty meters above people's heads. In Sitges you'll look up at it, this fountain, and you'll be penetrated by elation. You'll welcome it.

I can't stop talking about it:

"Of course, the newspapers allowed themselves to be provoked at first. It caused outrage and censure. They tried to drag Joan's name through the mud, and that made him laugh. I was the one who'd made the clay mock-up, the one we placed in the model of Sitges, surrounded by the square and the building's facades. We made a joint presentation to the heads of the town. The mayor sat there, looking serious and lost. 'A phallus. A phallus. A phallus!' he finally exclaimed, and for a few moments his face actually broke into an almost happy, if not sunny, expression. I'm trying to archive that image of the mayor in my mind, because he is almost always depicted in a dreary, newsprint sort of way, which makes you think he's a man without a face, and heart. The mayor, that is."

"I understand."

I decide to show him the clay miniature. I have one in iron too, which I cast and threaded a hose through so you can watch it gush.

"The day we presented it, we bought cava from the mayor's hometown. We hooked it up to the hose and let it rain on the chamber."

I'm laughing. But he looks grave.

I hurry to the kitchen. Salt-encrusted fish, lukewarm and still edible, and various salads.

"Are you sure you don't want a bite?"

"What about him? Are you sure he won't be coming home?"

"He never comes home on Fridays."

I had to stop myself from adding that he has meetings.

"So who did you cook for today? For me?"

"No, for him."

"But you said he doesn't come home on Fridays."

"You never know."

"I'm sorry, but this is hilarious. You're sitting there with dinner cooling on the stove while he's pleasuring himself with another woman. You're unbearable. He must hate you."

"We work together. We have a lot in common. And it's none of your business what I do in my solitude. Cooking is quite an innocent pursuit."

"I don't know about that."

He's getting drunk. When I fetch something from the kitchen or even move for the wine across the table, it's as though he's reaching for me.

"Tell me about him."

"Excuse me?"

"Tell me about him. I've been following him for so long, after all. Your husband walks very slowly, I'll tell you that for free – shadowing him takes patience. He stops to look at anything that moves; you'd think he were a kid if his age weren't so obvious."

"Your words, not mine."

"Don't be so la-di-da. Tell me about you. How you do it."

"What?"

"It."

"What?"

"Don't be coy. Tell me how you fuck."

"I think it's time for you to go. I'll get the checkbook."

"That can wait."

"You seem like a simple man. Drab and simple. You should leave."

"I don't think so."

"I'll call the police."

"Whore."

"John."

"Whore."

We laugh. We're drunk now. So drunk I knock over the wine bottle. The wine spills across the table and stains his pants.

"It happens," he says.

"You can't sit around like that. Wet."

"I guess I'll have to go home, then."

"You can borrow a pair of my husband's trousers. I'll go get a pair."

"I'll come with you. I haven't seen the view from the bedroom yet."

*

There's something about the light, how it moves as the buzz goes to my head. The sea turns a strange blue. The sea should be seen facing west, not like here: facing east. East is for dawn people. We are not dawn people. Not me, not the detective, not Joan.

"Cigar?"

"No, thank you."

"A bad habit my husband has after meals."

"You think about him all the time. And smile. It's like rain and raincoats with you – the truth can't get a foothold, doesn't get in, it just rolls right over the surface then evaporates."

I like him. I feel like telling him how I do it, and then asking him to tell me how he and his wife do it. Or he and his whoever. But he's earnest. It's like he's suddenly not in the mood anymore. I get on the bed, puffing the cigar and blowing smoke at the ceiling. I've always liked seeing smoke from this perspective. Dispersing at the ceiling. Spreading in small ringed clouds, like an atom bomb in miniature.

"Does he smoke in bed?"

"Who?"

"Your husband."

"He smokes where he wants. In bed, in the bathroom, and the kitchen."

"And the butts . . . ?"

"On the floor."

"And you follow him around, sweeping up."

It's the liquor, it's the whole situation, it's the fountain: the elation inside me won't sink. It rises and falls like a wave. And the hand grabs for me again, searching, methodical. That's the kind of man he is, the detective. Methodical in his work, and perhaps a little loving.

"Tell me about how they do it. My husband and her."

"What?"

"How they fuck, of course."

I'm laughing at myself: imagine, me, talking like this! And he tells me. Soon I want to drag myself out of my stupor – it needles now, right as I was getting to a safe place.

"Wait."

The idea comes from the drink, yes, it does, because we can't deny we're drunk now the wine bottle is empty and some of the pear cognac has been drained from the potbellied bottle. The report is on the coffee table, shut, the cover stamped with rings from the wineglasses. Of course, it would have been more appropriate for me to sit there, commenting on his work and allowing myself to be cocooned in gloom.

Appropriate. That's a funny word. Where did that come from?

"I have to show you the fountain in action."

I open the closet and take out the iron model, get a bottle of cava from the refrigerator, go into the bathroom and uncork the bottle, stick in the hose, and push the button. The cava sprays the entire bathroom.

"Look!" I shout. Now he's laughing, too.

I raise the bottle, put it to his mouth. I drink. I wind the hose around his wrists. His lips look kissable. He says no one has ever put him in bondage before. He doesn't have a lot of hair, is mostly bald. His breath is sour. He is disgusting.

I tug at him.

"Let's play a game. Come on. Lie on your belly. Bend your knees, put your feet to your ass. Like that. Hands tied behind your back, then a hose around your ankles and the same hose around your neck. It's a fun game. Lie still."

He obeys. He must be quite drunk. He was nice while he was letting me talk about the business with the no man's land. He was nice for a while after that, too, but now it's as if the niceness has vanished and been replaced with the quality I didn't like from the start.

I sit on the toilet, flipping through the report.

"The report is bizarre. There's a lot that disturbs me here."

"Sure, let's talk about it. But take the rope off."

"You mean the hose."

"Yes, take the hose off. I thought this was a game."

"This is a game."

"Yes, but when does it start?"

"It's not one of those games. Let's talk about the report."

"You have to take the rope off."

"The hose."

"The hose. You have to take the hose off. It's strangling me every time I relax."

"Yes. That's the game."

"Take it off. I can't handle it anymore. I have to vomit. I'm drunk."

"As I said, I think the report is bizarre."

"It's just a normal report, for Christ's sake."

"There are too many pictures. I think it puts my husband and his lover in a bad light."

"Isn't that what you want?"

"Why would I want that?"

"Because you've been spurned! I just did what I thought you wanted. Why hire a detective if you don't want the truth? Why did you want me to deliver it in person if you didn't want sympathy?"

*

The light in the bathroom is moving. Reflected light pounces across the shower curtain. In spite of the baldness and the corpulence, his voice is shrill. I don't like his voice.

I crawl in between the wall and the toilet. Cover my ears. Belt out a song I learned in school. It's about fish who drink up their own river, drinking and drinking as they're swimming around in the water. Meanwhile, the Virgin Mary is combing her hair at the water's edge. Why is she combing her hair at the edge of the water and why are the fish drinking their own river?

I start rocking, I can't help it, he must think I'm crazy. Joan must be coming home soon. The last plane from Madrid has left, contrails drawn across the sky. I should clear the table. Should tidy up. Gather myself, but there's something else inside me, too, a new no man's land. It's what's spreading inside me – I'm the gauze, and the no man's land is the ink I'm soaking up. I take my hands from my ears and scream that at him, that I am the gauze and I'm absorbing this land now, and I can't stop and I can't help him until it's done. Doesn't he understand? Doesn't he see that I'm suffering, too? It's not enough that I'm suffering – I'm paralyzed. So paralyzed I can't set him free. I get this way sometimes. It's not my fault, it just happens, it's a part of me.

Silence, finally. One of those audible silences, one of those silences where I don't dare open my eyes. I fall asleep, but not before telling myself to drink three glasses of water, otherwise the headache will be blinding and my eyes will be like gravel.

*

Joan's steps on the stairs wake me. The no man's land is gone, and I almost feel a lightness. The bathroom door opens and I see his shoes. He's standing there, silent.

Then he puts his hand on my head, and it is large and hot and caressing.

"Darling," he says. "Not again."

MAURICE ECHEGARAY

This happened when we were living off the southbound highway. Our apartment shared a stairwell with Maurice Echegaray's office, and there were three doors between his and ours. If Mom ran into him on the stairs, he'd complain about the cooking smell from the apartments seeping into his office through the vents. Mom said she wasn't about to stop eating just so he could sell whatever it was he was selling. Sometimes he gave me looks. Sometimes I stubbed my cigarette out by his door. There was a sign on it: *Maurice Echegaray Trade Management*. The sign was made of gold plastic, and if you pressed your nose to it, it smelled synthetic. Once, he flung open his door on me. Said: You creep, you're following me. You wish, I said, and he said excuse me and I repeated myself: You wish.

And that was it. He just watched me go, and his silhouette was slender in the light from the stairwell's window. From then on, when I met him in the entryway or in the garage he was always wary of me, like I was vermin or just any old bug.

Otherwise, not much used to happen in our stairwell back then. Two days a week an old lady came to clean. One time a pipe burst and the floor flooded. If you said that to one of those old ladies on the stairs, I mean if you said to them that there wasn't much going on here, they'd say things never *stopped* going on: our neighborhood used to be full of sheep stalls, orange groves, and an old porcelain factory that so-and-so's old man had worked in when he was young. Then the cranes arrived. New facades, shiny facades, facades that reflected the sky. Price Waterhouse, Inditex, Iberia. On the rooftops were green oases with pools for the employees, who were bank directors, consultants, and other smooth operators.

"Up there, the traffic sounds like the ocean," my friend Isabel told me. She'd been up there once. "You can lie on a deck chair, drink a margarita, and pretend you're in the Bahamas, but really it's just Valencia."

Dad said it was nice to live here now. With all the new developments, the neighborhood was really coming up.

"I don't know about 'nice,'" Mom said. "The new parts are quite nice, but what we have is actually quite ugly."

And she was right. From the balcony, you could see our house reflected by the new, and that mirror image set the defects in sharp relief. Discolored and washed-out clothes hung on laundry lines strung across the balconies. Bricks showed through the plaster. The awnings gave a pop of color, but exhaust fumes had turned their orange grimy. It was difficult to understand why Price Waterhouse would set up shop across from a building like ours, in the same way that it was difficult to understand why someone like Maurice Echegaray wanted an office in our building. Or why someone would put a gym here. It was on the ground floor of the building across from us and had a Turkish bath and an ice machine with ice chips to rub on your skin. No cellulite in the world was a match for that, according to the people who worked there. When the gym's doors slid open, the smell of luxury wafted out onto the street, which otherwise mostly smelled of exhaust fumes and burnt earth. You could stand outside those doors, inhaling that scent of luxury, but someone would eventually come along and tell you to make up your mind: are you in or out?

It was only after the ad appeared in the newspaper that I had a chance to really get to know Maurice Echegaray. The very same week I graduated high school: *Maurice Echegaray Trade Management Seeking Qualified Personnel.*

"Will you look at that," Dad said. "The Frenchman is expanding."

"What a coincidence," I told Isabel. "The very same week I'm graduating."

I called the number in the ad. An answering machine picked up, and a mechanical voice said that Maurice Echegaray couldn't be reached. I said my name was Almudena Reyes. I lived three doors away and could imagine working for Maurice Echegaray if the pay was halfway decent. He could call me, or stop by if he preferred. I thought about adding something about my education, but the beep interrupted me and calling back felt silly.

I waited. Summer was on its way, and the thermometers on the street read twenty-nine degrees. Haze veiled the sky. In the evenings the cockroaches ran in and out of the drains, and sometimes we chased them, trying to smash them with a shoe, and when we succeeded, there was a crunch and then a dark stain on the sole.

Maurice Echegaray didn't call back. Nor did he stop by. I applied for other jobs, too, but they didn't get back to me either. I waited a whole week, and then halfway through the second week I rang his doorbell.

"I'd like to work here," I said when he opened the door.

"I don't need any help," he replied.

"It said you did in the paper."

Maurice Echegaray fixed his eyes on me. His nose was crooked, his skin dark. His white suit had a silky sheen, and he was wearing gold-plated cuff links. There was a whiff of expensive perfume around us. Then he let me in. The apartment was the same as ours: you walked into a small hall and the living room was straight ahead. There was a set of black leather sofas that looked kind of sticky, backlit from the street.

"You've grown up," he said.

"Yes," I said.

We talked for a while. About the building in general, the neighbors and their children, the cranes and how hard it was to find a job nowadays, how no one was lining up to hire anyone. Then we sat in silence. You could hear someone walking around upstairs, water rushing through a pipe.

"I only employ professionals," he finally said.

He clasped his hands in his lap. Crossed his legs.

"I see," I said.

"Them's the breaks."

I said I was a quick study. All my teachers had said so: I had potential.

"Would you call yourself a pro?" Maurice Echegaray asked.

"No," I said. "Not a pro. I'm saying that because I prefer not to lie, especially to myself."

That line usually hits home with people, but Maurice Echegaray shook his head and said it was a shame I didn't like lying because in business, lying was essential. Essential.

And if you could manage to lie to yourself, that was even better, as far as believability goes.

"But maybe you can learn," he said. "If you have so much potential."

Silence again. He asked me if I wanted coffee, and I said no. He asked me if I wanted a glass of water, and I said yes. He left the room and came back with a glass of water that tasted of chlorine.

"I need someone to answer the phone," he said. "And since you already live next door, well."

I shrugged. An answering service. That was nothing to brag about, really. Though you could start at the bottom and work your way up. Some people do that: they get in at the ground floor and end up top dog. So I said yes, and we agreed I would start the next day, and if there was anything else he needed help with, I said, all he had to do was shout. The telephone hadn't rung once that entire time.

I had been right about the phone, it didn't make a sound. The first afternoon went by slowly; I mostly listened to Maurice Echegaray talking on the phone in his office. His voice came through the half-open office door. Sometimes it sounded upbeat, sometimes it sounded angry. When he was angry, he spoke slowly, overarticulating each syllable, as though he were speaking to an idiot. I eavesdropped a lot, but mostly I was bored. I got acquainted with the office. The black leather sofas were still shabby, and upon closer inspection the place was actually pretty messy. I emptied ashtrays and vacuumed. I watered the flowers and saw that he'd stubbed out his cigarettes in the pots, too. I cleaned the toilet, and on the mirror I used a blue spray I'd found in the cleaning closet which stank of ammonia. Then I aired the place out, created a through breeze, got rid of the stale air, even if the air that came in was hot and nauseating.

When Maurice Echegaray was leaving for the day, he said:

"It looks nice in here. Just pull the door shut when you leave."

I waited until the door closed behind him. Then I went into his office, opened the drawers, and found his cigarettes. I sat on his chair and put my feet up on the table. I sat like that for a while, leaning my head against the headrest and looking out the window. You could see the Price Waterhouse logo across the way, mirrored glass, and a bit of sky, patterned with contrails. I drew the smoke into my throat, coughed, and put the cigarette out in the newly emptied ashtray.

Then I stowed the vacuum in the cleaning closet, poured out the mop water in the toilet, and went home to my mother, who asked how my first day at work was.

Over a few months, Maurice Echegaray and I built up a kind of routine. I would arrive in the morning, fiddle with the pots or whatever in the office, and then sit at my desk chatting with Isabel. Sometimes a call came in and I would answer it, putting the caller through to Maurice Echegaray. Midmorning, we'd go down to the bar in the building across the way. We'd sit at a table on the sidewalk, and often Maurice Echegaray would wear black sunglasses in which I could see my reflection. My nose looked big in those glasses, deformed and wide. People would look at him with curiosity and a touch of fear. You could see that in his glasses, too, in the lenses. He spoke loudly, and when something upset him his gestures would become quite grand. Once, he said he might not be God's favorite child, but he had a good relationship with life itself. I didn't understand what he meant by that, but I nodded anyway. He also said he thought I was doing a good job and there was a container of swim caps on its way in, maybe I could handle those when the time came. He said I had been right at the job interview, I did have potential, and if everything went well he would make me a consultant. Teach me a thing or two about trade. Make sure I earned some money and had some fun in this old life.

At home, I said I was doing a sort of apprenticeship, and I would soon have a chance to test my mettle.

"Very good," Mom said.

In retrospect, maybe I should've taken advantage of those early days of our emerging routine. Change is the only constant. Everybody says that, I guess, but understanding it is another thing, really understanding it, from the inside, so to speak.

"I've hired a professional now," he announced a few weeks later.

We were down in the bar and he was leaning against the wall, smoking.

"A pro?" I said.

"Yep. A real pro."

He explained that when he'd placed the ad in the newspaper it had been someone like that he was after. Someone who knew how it's done. Someone competent. Who had a nose for these things.

I said that I hoped it was a nice person and wondered what he was called.

"It's no he," said Maurice. "It's a girl. A lady. A woman."

*

She was called Rebeca. I found her standing in the office the next day. The first thing I saw when I came in that morning was her petite, high-heeled silhouette against the window.

"Rebeca, Almudena. Almudena, Rebeca," said Maurice, and we coolly kissed each other on the cheek.

It didn't take me long to see that Rebeca and I could never work together. She was just that type, provocative down to the tiniest pore. She'd saunter around the office, holding her cigarette low, ashing on the floor. She crossed her arms when she talked to anyone, and if you disagreed with her she asked if you were prepared to discuss it. After a few days, there was ash all over the apartment. I tried to restrain myself. I told her it was "impractical" for her to ash on the floor.

"Why?" she said. "It's marble. It won't make any holes."

Her eyes were dark. When you looked into their depths, it was like something was there at the bottom. Something cold and muscular, like a fish, or an eel.

"Rebeca," Maurice Echegaray said to me. "She can sell anything. Exhaust systems, cans of bait, shampoo, and manure by the kilo. She lands it in no time."

That's where she was misleading him, I thought. She was the manipulative, shit-talking type. She'd come here, stubbing out cigarettes to mark her territory, and probably had her sights set on Maurice Echegaray.

Still, one month on I had to give him some credit, because Rebeca's sales were gaining momentum. She stayed until late at night, making phone calls, sorting out the customs declarations. In the mornings she'd be down at the harbor, making sure the cranes were handling her containers right, because if you didn't, she said, they seemed to drop them in the gap between the boat and the dock on purpose, and in addition to the goods being ruined you had to start the whole process from the top, and that right there was the hinterland of insurance.

"Listen and learn," Maurice Echegaray told me.

I listened. And I learned.

"We've quadrupled our takings since Rebeca arrived," Maurice Echegaray said after a while. "That woman knows how it's done, I'll say it again, she knows how it's done."

"I'm getting cellulite," Isabel said at some point in all this.

I told her about the ice machine at the gym.

"Way too expensive," she said.

"Try it at home, then," I said. "It must work with regular ice from the freezer, too."

The phone in the office was ringing a lot now. Most calls were for Rebeca, and I didn't have time to clean anymore. Soon Rebeca's debris covered the floor. I would sit at my desk eating my packed lunch and stare at the ash on the floor, wondering how anyone could carry on like that. What century were we living in? Expecting people to clean up after you.

"Do you feel like tidying up tonight?" Maurice Echegaray asked one day.

"Everything but Rebeca's mess," I said.

"Don't be like that," Maurice said.

I didn't reply. I fiddled with the keypad on the phone even though the handset was in the cradle. I made a mound of the crumbs from my packed lunch.

"What do you want in exchange?" he asked.

"What do you mean?"

"How can I compensate you? What do you want for the trouble?"

"Tell me a secret," I said.

"What kind of secret?" he wondered.

"A secret you've never told anyone else. Here at the office."

He laughed. Went into the kitchen, and I heard him handling the jar of instant coffee. The kettle hissed. Then he came back with a cup of coffee.

"I have a hole in my heart," he said.

He was leaning against the doorframe. He said it with that French accent of his and looked at me. There was something playful in his eyes, and it was hard to say if he was kidding or just happy. I thought about suggesting we go to the beach. To talk about the hole in his heart. I usually did that with Isabel, went to the beach I mean, and it was always nice, even if there were a lot of large, loose poops lying around. Made by children and dogs. Sometimes the wind covered them with sand and if you stepped on one it squished up between your toes, covering your nails, like the sand does when the waves pull back from the shore.

But Maurice got there before me:

"I have to run," he said and put his coffee cup on the windowsill. "I'll be seeing you."

"OK," I said.

I vacuumed. Cleaned the bathroom, used furniture spray. Thought about the beach, wondered if he'd been there, if he knew Valencia at all, and how I could bring it up again. When I was finished cleaning, I sat in Maurice Echegaray's chair and opened his drawers. In one was a packet of Lucky Strikes, and next to it was a pack of Puros Canteros. I opened it and took out a cigar, lit it, and put my feet up on the desk. I took easy, deep puffs, even though I'd heard you're not supposed to inhale cigar smoke. Then I went into Rebeca's office and did the same thing there. Maybe this was twisted, well, not twisted but maybe not normal. I remembered Isabel telling me that one of her mother's friends was a cleaner who worked until everything was spick-and-span but when she was done, she pulled down her pants and peed on the edge of the toilets. A little on each toilet seat, running through each floor again even though she was done for the day and could have just gone home to her family. I mean, only not normal compared to *that*.

I walked across the floor like Rebeca did, with my hand on my hip, waiting for the ash to fall. But cigars burn slowly, and the ash is compact. I ended up having to tap it off with my index finger, and then the flakes sailed slowly down. I looked for a pattern in the ash that would tell me the future or more about Maurice Echegaray, then I took out the vacuum cleaner, sucked up the dirt, and went home for the day.

It got hotter. The air was heavy with exhaust fumes. Rebeca said there was a kind of fog over Valencia. Not just in the summer, but always. An orange-grove fog, and she said it was inside the people too, giving rise to a certain kind of temperament. Stolid and somewhat flat. If she thought about it, she said, she'd never been in a city as stolid as Valencia. I didn't respond. I've heard it before, and I know it's something people say when they come here because they're jealous and can't think of anything else to say.

It was after vacation, sometime in late summer, that Maurice Echegaray said it was time to move offices. Thanks to Rebeca's efforts – that's how he put it – we were able to upgrade to the building across the street. The Price Waterhouse building, the Inditex building – and yes, the gym building. There, each one of us would have our own little office, and there would be no fuss over the view because the place was on the seventeenth floor. Only a few formalities remained, he said. The mortgage. But he would sort that out tomorrow at the bank, and there would be no problem because they knew him, saw him every day down at the bar.

But the next day he didn't mention the bank or the loan and it made me wonder but I didn't want to ask. In the evening, Dad told me what had happened at the bank.

"I have news," he began.

Pedro Fraga, the bank manager, had told him Maurice Echegaray had made a scene at the bank when he came in to ask about a mortgage for his new office, which was to be in the same high-rise as the gym, and which the bank's real estate department would need to administer. The bank had denied his loan application. Dad didn't know why, but he said that if the bank refused to grant a mortgage, the bank had its reasons.

"Echegaray lost it," Dad said, whipping his hands in the air.

He'd accused the bank of being nationalists. Fraga said he'd said it in such a funny way, *Spanish nationalists through and through*, in a priceless French accent that made matters worse, that made it impossible to take Echegaray seriously.

"Ah well," said Dad. "Then he went on his way, that Echegaray."

Striding out of the bank, strutting, Dad added, but Fraga must have put those words in his mouth because I'd never seen Maurice Echegaray strut. You could almost turn it around and say if there was one person who didn't strut, it was Maurice Echegaray.

But it didn't end there, according to Dad. The next day, something truly sensational happened. Echegaray came back into the bank, hoisted a briefcase onto the bank manager's desk, and said:

"Voilà!"

They opened the briefcase. Counted it out, checked the notes. One million euros. It made you wonder where the money came from. Fraga asked Echegaray outright, and Echegaray told Fraga to forget about it. Forget about it, he said, *royalement,* forget about it. Fraga found out a thing or two. And the conclusion was Maurice had contacts in the underworld, possibly with the Nigerians. Of all the Africans, Nigerians were the worst. They set up networks, played with loaded dice. This was a known fact, Fraga said, suggesting Dad should think twice about where I was working so I didn't get mixed up in "irregularities." People in the neighborhood were going to be keeping an eye on Echegaray's affairs.

"Maybe he's involved with drugs and prostitution," Mom said.

She smoothed her worried hands over her apron, mumbling that at night all cats were leopards and I should make sure not to get dragged into anything that had anything to do with Nigerians.

I went to my room. Tried to remember if I'd seen strange things in Maurice Echegaray's desk drawers. But I couldn't remember having seen anything but cigarettes and cigars and a Waterman pen, so I put the whole thing out of my mind, thinking he'd get his loan and Fraga would probably calm down eventually.

*

"That ice machine is superb," said Isabel. "I've gotten rid of it all now."

"Your cellulite?" I asked.

"Yes. Want to try?"

I shrugged, saying it was expensive.

"What you invest in yourself now," Isabel said, "will come back to you in the future."

I started working out. Going to the gym every day after work, lying in the Turkish bath or on the sun terrace. Sometimes I swam in the pool, and one day I ran into Rebeca.

"You!" we said at the same time.

That was about it. I went to the hot tub and she went to the ice machine. I kept my eye on her, tracking her when she got up and waiting to make sure I wouldn't run into her in the changing room. But clearly I didn't wait long enough, because when I went in she was sitting on the bench, washed and dressed. Beside her, her bag was closed.

"You took forever," she said.

"I didn't know you were waiting," I replied.

She sat there looking at me. I knotted the towel around my waist and dried my hair. I didn't like her looking at me.

When my hair was dry and it was time to change, I said:

"Why are you staring at me?"

"I want to see if you have cellulite," she said.

My God, I thought. I took my clothes into a bathroom stall and changed. When I emerged, she said:

"You don't like me."

I shrugged.

"I might not like you, you might not like me. Is that a problem?"

"No," she said.

She got up and came closer to me.

"Do you think I've gained weight?" she said.

I shook my head.

"But look here," she said and pulled up her skirt. "If it's not fat, then what is it?"

She grabbed one of her butt cheeks, squeezing it together so hard the skin folded.

"Isn't this the beginning of cellulite? Tell me."

"That's orange-peel skin," I said.

"And what is that?"

"The step before cellulite. That's when it's called orange peel."

She let her skirt drop.

"I see. Do you have it, too?"

"No."

"Let me see."

"No."

"Let me see. Oh my God, Almudena, don't be ridiculous. Woman to woman, whether or not we like each other, you can show me your cellulite!"

I sat on the bench and pressed my knees together.

"You're stingy with yourself," Rebeca said.

She gave a theatrical sigh.

"And I get the feeling that Maurice hates cellulite."

"Maurice Echegaray?" I asked.

I must've sounded wounded, because her smile was victorious. She slung her bag over her shoulder and made for the door.

I really should have been happy in spite of it all. The container with the swim caps arrived, and I was going to rise up the office ranks. I was going to learn a thing or two about trade, and Maurice would hire someone else to answer the phone and tidy up. If anyone had told me a year ago I'd be working for Maurice Echegaray and rising through the ranks and someone would be answering my calls for me, I'd hardly have believed my ears. I would've thought my future lay ahead of me like a freshly raked beach. But when the moment finally came, my stomach was in knots. I didn't know anything about swim caps or containers, and Rebeca was the one who was supposed to train me, which couldn't possibly end well, if you asked me.

The girl who was supposed to answer the phone was called Sonsoles. I was supposed to train her. It probably wouldn't take very long, Maurice had said, because it was mostly just pushing buttons and sounding friendly.

"It's important," he said, "to make sure she doesn't chew gum and is friendly to the clients. There's no telephone etiquette here in Spain."

I told Sonsoles, who had a large mouth and smelled of strawberry, and she nodded and spat in the wastebasket. I added that Rebeca had the bad habit of ashing on the floor and I'd gone around wiping it up for almost six months, and now it was Sonsoles' turn.

"OK," said Sonsoles.

I took my notepad and went into Rebeca's office. She was leaning back in her chair, holding a Waterman pen between her thumb and index finger. She said that the world of trade was the real world. You had to be good-looking and proper and sure of yourself, but not strange.

"OK," I said, wondering which drawer she kept the Waterman pen in and imagining holding it myself the next time I sat in her chair.

And then there were a number of procedures, she said, but those I could google. Credit agreements, terms of delivery, and such. Each product was a world unto itself. One day you were selling timber, the next exhaust pipes. If you made a loss, you just had to pick yourself up and move on. As far as the swim caps were concerned, brainstorming was the most important part.

"Brainstorm," she said. "Who could use a swim cap?"

Her telephone rang and she shooed me off like you would a fly. My lesson was over, and I went back to my spot, thinking about who could use a swim cap. My first thought was public pools, but the few I called said they already had their suppliers and they weren't exactly big consumers. Next, I called manufacturers of toiletry bags, but they didn't want any either.

"I saw swim caps at El Corte Inglés," Mom said when I told her over dinner.

Maurice and Rebeca laughed when I told them.

"The big fish," they said, sarcastically. "Sure, why not? I'm sure they'd love to buy swim caps from Almudena Reyes."

What a rotten thing to say. But the rottenest thing was they were right, because swim caps were impossible to sell, and the operator at Corty just kept passing me around until I got dizzy and hung up. I asked Maurice for another product, and it took a lot to do that. I felt foolish for suffering such a clear defeat.

"Of course people buy swim caps," Rebeca snapped. "You just have to get through to the right channels. Use your brain."

She smiled as she said it, and it occurred to me that this was probably the first time I'd seen her teeth. After that I called Corty five days a week, five times a day. Each time the lady at the operator desk said that I should speak with one Asunción, but she was very busy and almost never there.

"Then I'll keep on calling, if that's all right," I said.

"You do that," said the woman at the operator desk.

I talked about swim caps at home. Mom and Dad said it was nice that I was working, but was a job worth having if you couldn't leave it at the door when you came home? Isabel asked me how it was going. I said it was going well. That Maurice Echegaray was a business genius who could sell practically anything. And me, the hub of his wheel. We were a dynamic duo and if it hadn't been for Rebeca everything would have been fine, but I suppose every paradise has its snake.

One day Asunción was there.

"I'll connect you," her secretary said.

I said my name was Almudena Reyes, and I was calling from Maurice Echegaray Trade Management. I wanted to come by and show her samples of swim caps. They came in every color and were a steal.

It was quiet on the line. Then she said:

"You sound nervous."

I took a second to search for a good response. Until finally she said with a sigh:

"Come by tomorrow at eleven o'clock. I'll give you fifteen minutes."

"Impossible," said Maurice Echegaray when I returned to the office the following day.

Even Rebeca came out of her office to listen to Maurice and Sonsoles congratulate me. She looked away and ashed on the floor. I told her I wasn't cleaning up around here anymore, Sonsoles was the one taking care of the cigarette butts now. Rebeca nodded and leaned against the doorway, and there was the eel, cold and writhing around at the bottom of her gaze.

A few weeks later we moved into the new office. We could see the inland orange groves and the sea from our windows. I looked for the old porcelain factory but saw no chimneys overgrown with grass, so maybe they'd already torn it down. There were cream leather sofas in the middle of the space. On the table was a large green bowl filled with pistachios. Sonsoles received calls, and I occasionally went down to the bar and picked up coffee. There was wall-to-wall carpeting, so Rebeca wasn't allowed to ash on the floor anymore, Maurice Echegaray said. Fraga called from the bank almost every day. Now that Echegaray had bought the apartment with cash, it could act as a security for other things. Building insurance, health insurance, accident insurance, life insurance. Child insurance, if he'd had children. White goods and leased cars. A Volvo? A Jeep?

"All successful people have a Jeep nowadays," Fraga said.

And Maurice Echegaray laughed, because that's how it is with flattery, it always works and if it doesn't it's because you're not laying it on thick enough. I knew because I was standing with my hand in the pistachio bowl, listening to Fraga tinkering with Maurice like a mechanic tinkers with a car engine. Finally, Maurice was up and running, purring along, in the palm of Fraga's hand, and when Fraga gave it some gas, Maurice gave it some gas too. Soon, he bought a large black Jeep that Sonsoles dreamily described as masculinity incarnate. Maurice Echegaray, he said it was mostly for fun. A company car, two, in case he needed to make company visits. And Rebeca, the golden calf, was given hers. A car and a gift card so she could kit herself out with the wardrobe that was "called for in her profession."

I was given nothing.

"But your time will come," said Maurice Echegaray. "Now that you're rolling along with the swim caps, there'll be more, and when you start keeping up with Rebeca I'm going to make sure you get a car *and* a wardrobe."

And in any case, I couldn't complain because everything was going quite well. Asunción called and said she needed four more containers of swim caps over the next year. Payment in advance and no haggling over the price. On this occasion Maurice bought a bottle of cava, and we toasted in the office. I asked if he remembered the time he'd called me a creep. That was a long time ago, he said. A lot of water had run under the bridge since then. Now I was someone else. A professional, flogging swim caps like no other. I wanted to say something about his heart. Was having a hole in it dangerous, was it large or small? I wanted to tell him the beach was nice this time of year, that all of a sudden they were cleaning it up with a tractor twice a day, you could walk there, and it was a part of Valencia I'd be happy to show him if he had the time and inclination.

But I was too shy to bring up his heart. And shyness was not the way to go, because Rebeca was showing fresh determination, and it was with Maurice Echegaray as it was with her products: once her heart was set on something, she got it. There had been indications. Like when they bought rollerblades and did a test run in the office. Rebeca already knew how to skate and glided elegantly between the potted plants and marble tables. Maurice stumbled behind her like a gangly calf, pulling down folders and piles of paper for recycling when he stumbled. Sonsoles followed behind, clearing up. I said I thought this was frivolous, that we were here to sell, not amuse ourselves like five-year-olds.

Rebeca and Maurice began to withdraw. They would stay away from the office for several days at a time. When they came back, Maurice would be in high spirits. You could already hear Rebeca out in the hall, loud and excited. But when she caught sight of us in the office, it was always the same. Her face would go stiff, she'd cross her arms, and the eel would settle in her gaze, then she'd go into her office and close the door behind her. If you ever said anything about them being late or wondered where they'd been, she'd reply that the business was running well enough for us not to worry about it. You couldn't argue. The neighborhood was calling Maurice Echegaray a sales whiz, a jet-setter. Dad said he was now one of the bank's most important clients, that Fraga could pay half his salaries with the income his operations alone pulled in. And still, Fraga suspected that the morals were loose at our office. That there were connections to the underworld. Dealings — Fraga could probably put two and two together. A steady influx of containers and a lump sum of one million euros. These things were strung together — by invisible, fine, crisscrossing threads that no one could see, but which made people stumble and fall, never to rise again.

But I didn't really care much about that, to be honest. Invisible threads, Dad and Fraga scheming over vermouth in the bar next to the bank — no, I had other things on my mind. The swim caps were selling like hotcakes. I couldn't believe the market wasn't getting saturated, that people really could buy that many swim caps. Asu called and ordered more, paid when her truck driver picked up the containers in the harbor, and I waited down there like Rebeca did, pointing and screaming at the dock workers, telling them to be careful with my particular containers. In the office, we always had cava and finger sandwiches in the refrigerator, because the way we were selling now, we needed to raise a toast almost every day. Yes, it went so far as Maurice Echegaray and Rebeca getting engaged. When I heard the news, I thought that if everything was going to sour, it would be now that they were engaged, because they sort of lost their judgment around each other. They were happy, oblivious to their surroundings, not at all on guard. The eel in Rebeca's eyes never turned up anymore, and sometimes they were out of the office for days. When I called Maurice Echegaray at home, they came right out and said they'd been in bed for days and might turn up at the office sometime next week.

We could manage ourselves, they said.

"Almudena and her swim caps," I heard Rebeca shout in the background.

"Make sure Sonsoles doesn't stick too much gum under the table," Maurice Echegaray said.

It was all about the two of them now. I couldn't help but wonder: if I'd been quicker to suggest the beach, instead of deliberating, would things be different?

"They suit each other really well," said Sonsoles. "I'm not sure I've ever seen a more handsome couple."

On one of those days, a friend of Maurice Echegaray's stopped by the office. He introduced himself as Smart, and he was black as the night. He said there was a problem with some containers. They'd found objects inside them. At customs.

"What kind of objects?" I asked.

Smart shrugged. Said he wasn't sure, but his customs contact had said Maurice Echegaray best get ready. They might search the premises if they had misgivings.

I made a call, and soon Maurice and Rebeca were at the office, picking up their briefcases and then heading to the harbor. They didn't come back that afternoon, and the rumor spread. When I went home for lunch Dad said Fraga had been informed about "irregularities" down at the harbor, they'd found a thing or two in Echegaray's containers.

"But what?" I asked.

"Rocks and African weapons," Dad said.

"Hold up," I said. "No one gets put away for a few rocks and knives."

"It's the principle," Dad said. "Those jet-setters think the rules don't apply to them. That's what Fraga doesn't like, the principle."

The principle.

I thought about the principle.

The next afternoon the rumor spread all the way up the stairwell. Echegaray had been arrested down at the harbor. Couldn't be remanded in custody yet, but it was only a matter of time. People whispered. When they went up on the terrace to take down their sheets, women stopped to speak in low voices, "exchanging information," they called it.

By dinnertime the whole building was on its feet. The old men, who otherwise mostly just sat around watching television, were up too. Standing down by the mailbox and talking about Maurice Echegaray's contraband, smoking and putting his cigarettes out on the floor.

I went grocery shopping, assuming that Maurice would probably be back at the office in a few hours and would be exhausted.

I bought a lobster. It wasn't like I knew how to prepare one, but I could ask Mom on my way back. Going from the market to our house, I noticed that something had changed. It took a while for me to put my finger on it, but then there it was. The balconies were full of people. Everyone was sitting outside – old men and old ladies and children. Families had come out, cleared away the mops and cleaning supplies that normally filled their balconies, and were sitting there, as though they were waiting for something. Eating, they were eating of course. But it was the first time I'd ever seen the people from our building dining on the balconies, and they looked funny, misplaced, and a bit awkward. Like expectant caged hens, or like any animal kept in stacked cages.

Mom told me how to prepare the lobster. Said all you had to do was stick it in the pressure cooker, turn the screws, and let it die. Then she informed me that she and Dad were going to have their dinner on the balcony.

"But why?" I asked.

"It's a fine evening," said Mom.

"What about all the clouds?" I replied.

"Oh," said Mom. "It'll be a while before they reach us. And anyway," she said, lowering her voice, "I'd very much like to see what that jet-setter looks like when he comes back. Him and the dark one. The prostitute!"

I shut the door behind me and rejoined Sonsoles, who couldn't believe her ears either.

We set the table with a red cloth that Sonsoles had fetched from home. The wine was chilling. When the lobster moved inside the white plastic bag, Sonsoles looked disgusted. I tried to put her at ease, telling her how fresh it was.

Soon it was nine o'clock, nine thirty, ten. By the time eleven rolled around, we decided to go out on the balcony to check on my building. Yes.

"No way," said Sonsoles. "They're still sitting there."

They were smoking and pouring wine, and you could hear the buzz of their conversation.

"It should always be like this," Sonsoles said. "It's, like, genial."

"Genial?" I said.

The sky was almost black, but we moved our chairs out anyway. We said we didn't want to miss this, people's reaction to Maurice Echegaray and Rebeca returning. That is, not the return of Rebeca and Maurice, but people's reaction to Maurice and Rebeca's return, we made this clear to each other and nodded in agreement.

Soon the sky broke. It rumbled and flashed, and in the kitchen the lobster crept around in its bag.

At midnight, I boiled it.

"It's a big 'un," Sonsoles said when the water had heated up and a ruckus started up from inside the pot.

We covered our ears. But as soon as it was on the table, we sucked the juice from its extremities. Its flesh was loose, white, and soft, melting on our tongues and mixing well with the chilled white wine.

It was half past midnight when the black Jeep pulled up in front of the building. I leaned over to see. The doors opened and they came out. Maurice Echegaray, his jacket over his arm, looking tired. After he'd shut the car door he loosened his tie, took it off, opened the door again, and tossed it inside. Rebeca came out of the car holding her shoes. The drains couldn't swallow all the rain, and the cobbles were flooded. On the balconies, I could see my neighbors, dead silent and staring at the street. It was nighttime, and probably never a particularly noisy time for traffic, but still, you could have heard a pin drop.

"Maurice," said Rebeca. "Let's dance."

Her voice echoed strangely between the buildings. She splashed around in a puddle, and even the splashing seemed to echo.

"Dance? Now?" he asked.

"Yes. Come on."

And Maurice Echegaray opened the car door for the third time, turned on the radio, and there was music playing. Low but audible, something slow. They took hold of each other and danced with their feet immersed in water. Our building was hushed. I don't think anyone dared breathe while they were out there. Then they locked the car and came up to the office, briefcases tucked under their arms, shoes dangling from their hands.

The building was uneasy the next day. I felt it as soon as I woke up, before I'd even opened my eyes: a sticky kind of despair was seeping from the walls.

"What makes people hate them the most," Mom said at breakfast, "isn't that they earn good money, it's that they act like they own the whole world. That's it. They act like they own the world."

Who else would ever come back in the middle of the night and treat our sidewalk like a dance floor? Did anyone else make a habit of driving their car halfway onto the sidewalk and parking just like that? Who among us even had a Jeep, which by the way practically took up two parking spots and really was just for people with an inferiority complex?

When it came down to it, not much had been found in the containers. A few African swords and some ivory bracelets, things that ended up in containers sometimes, nothing you'd turn the world upside down for, said customs. But Fraga declared he'd had enough. He couldn't do business with a person with an untrustworthy reputation, and he needed to be better informed about Maurice Echegaray's habits and economic situation. He called around. Checked with the authorities and various institutions, and then said he needed to collect general impressions of Maurice Echegaray in order to reach a truthful verdict. So he made house visits, and the snowball started rolling. People spoke, and Fraga made notes. Then he spent a few days deliberating in his office. Finally he stopped by our office and said he needed the loan he'd given Maurice Echegaray for cars, insurance, clothes, and apartments to be paid back in full.

"But you have the office as a guarantee," Maurice Echegaray said.

"That doesn't help," Fraga said. "I need the money now."

"But that's absurd."

"I'm asking for the money now," he said.

"We don't have the money now. So we'll have to move."

"That's not my problem," Fraga said, looking vulgar with his shiny forehead and pouting lips.

Fraga said he was sorry for me, he knew how much I liked my job and that I was doing well with the swim caps, but there would be other opportunities. Maybe even at his bank. Who knew? The future was a spectrum of unforeseeable opportunities.

I said nothing in reply. Nothing to Mom and Dad that evening. I didn't even say anything when Maurice and Rebeca stowed their computers in their briefcases and slammed the office door behind them, but I harbored a feeling that I couldn't share with anyone because it was chewy and stale, uninteresting and as empty as an old cupboard.

That was, by the way, the last time I saw Maurice Echegaray. A few days later a moving company carried out the sofas, desks, and computers. They were lugged into and out of the elevator, and we stood on the street, watching everything get loaded into a truck, which revved up and drove away — west toward Madrid, or maybe just out into the world.

MANY PEOPLE DIE LIKE YOU

It began in May. Vicente Jiménez took a pack of peas from the freezer counter, put them in his shopping cart, and promptly lost all sensation in his fingertips. It's the cold, he thought. You lose feeling. He carried on shopping. Spreading his hands and bending his fingertips, which were now pure white. Circulation issues. It happens, but if I think about something else the feeling will come back and I won't even remember it having gone. He drove home, dropped off the shopping, and continued to the university. He thought about that day's lectures. He would lead the students into the *Inferno*, focused and with a careful hand. While doing so, he'd think: I'm taking them down into the basement. And even further down. Then they'll see what's there. And what was there was always the same: people who'd loved each other and who'd fought for that love (Paolo and Francesca, Dido and Aeneas), battles for a love that was worthwhile. Jennifer, his favorite student and his lover, fixed her eyes on him when he talked about love, as though he were speaking of their own. He thought about the nape of her neck. The bitter taste of her skin at the hairline. He'd take off her jewelry and dangle her silver chain down between her breasts like a tiny snake, while asking if she'd done her homework. He pulled into

50

the department's parking lot. The sensation had returned to his fingertips, and the episode at the freezer counter had already been forgotten.

Even with the coming spring, this day was just like any other: dedicated to routine. He gave his lecture, met Jennifer's gaze, heard the scraping of chairs, and was left alone in the auditorium. The window was open, and he could hear the students' boom boxes blasting. A male voice rapped: *You're not eighteen. You are seventy-eight and the richest guy in some cemetery.* How was he supposed to teach Dante with that racket going on in the background? He called Jennifer. She was on the metro and sounded listless and distracted. He didn't understand. Hadn't things been good during the lecture? Still, he made an effort.

"Are you hungry?"

"I'm eating a kebab."

"Not that kind of hunger. Metaphors, Jennifer."

"Yeah. I know."

"Then I'll say it again: are you hungry?"

"Not hungry enough to eat spoiled meat."

The silver chain flashed before his eyes, sliding along her skin, toward her belly button, disappearing into it like a black hole. He gathered his papers and went home to Julia, who was in the kitchen, cooking. When he saw the pack of peas on the counter, a sudden pain coursed through his fingertips. They ate dinner together and fell asleep a few hours later, back-to-back in their marital bed, which was as wide as a boat. The silence around them was dense, and even though the spring night was pressing itself up against their windows, it did not manage to break into a single one of their dreams.

*

The next morning he walked down Pintor Rosales. The city was waking up, and its scents hit him in swells. Coffee, exhaust fumes, mop water from the stairwells being aired out, front doors open. Sweet, floral perfumes from the women in light clothing passing him by. He found this to be a lovely time of the year, a time when you wanted to be in love, and for that feeling to be mutual. But as the years went by, this equation became ever more difficult to square. Your standards were higher, but your life force was draining away. You became less attractive as you had less to give. Jennifer had said that, one night over a bottle of wine on Plaza Oriente. People's existential value diminished, if you took a Darwinian view. Of course, she'd intended it as a joke, but as she spoke the words seemed to captivate her, and she continued to share her thoughts with him, saying that at his age you weren't really contributing anything special.

"Are you saying I should roll over and die?" he'd asked.

"Look who's gone and gotten whiny," she'd replied. You didn't *have* to take a Darwinian view. *He* was contributing. He gave her a certain sexual satisfaction, for instance, plus he fed a lot of souls their daily manna. His existence was completely justified. She made a wise gesture with her arms.

A certain sexual satisfaction, he thought as he crossed Parque del Oeste. *Certain*. What did that word contain? A cooling-off? He passed by an orange machine sucking up last fall's leaves. He kicked a small stone on the path. His existence was completely justified, that's the thought he had to cling to, for a gut-wrenching pointlessness lay on the other side. Nourishing his students' minds, being generous with his flesh. Every day a spoonful of his flesh was fed to those hungry mouths, and the students gladly

52

ate of him. The keys to Dante, Cervantes, and Borges –
keys cut from his own flesh. Jennifer, in particular, was
happy to eat of him, like a little vampire, she listened
and learned. He should have watched out for this – it was
in the nature of things that she would eventually outwit
him. Her having the upper hand wasn't good for their
relationship. She wasn't the maternal type, Jennifer. Not
maternal at all. But before he met her he hadn't been in
love for a long time, an eternity, and his soul had been
as dry as tinder. For a moment he nudged up against the
thought that the last person he'd been in love with, before
Jennifer, was his wife. He batted the thought away. There
must have been somebody in between. He saw a blurred
face before him, a pair of lips slowly being painted rust-
red, a pair of thigh-highs on an otherwise naked body
and a hand reaching for him and pleading, or demanding,
that he give her money. Then the woman in his memory
cupped one breast. She was holding a pen in the other. She
wrote on her breast. It was his name. When she looked
up to meet his gaze he reached out his hand, but she
didn't take it. Instead she turned and walked away from
him. The thigh-highs digging in just below her rump, the
high heels making her hobble, she lumbered out of his
memory. He stopped on the gravel path and thought: It's
downhill for me. To be moved so intensely when otherwise
you hardly feel a thing. When he arrived at the steps of
the university, he had once again reached the conclusion
that in literature and dreams love is pure, but in reality,
it's dirty. And he satisfied himself with this truth for the
moment, checked his watch, and walked to Jerónimo
Inclán's office.

"Your melancholy is the most human of feelings,"
Jerónimo Inclán said when he told him the truth about

Jennifer and the hopelessness that was sinking its teeth in. "You must simply endure. At least spring is on its way."

He gestured at the window and the city outside and took a drag of his cigar, as though the subject had been settled.

"You don't understand," Vicente said. "I'm not sure I'm going to get over this."

"Lighten up."

They sat in silence for a while. Through the open window they could hear a boom box playing.

"Many people die like you," Inclán said then. "Death by stifling is in fact the most common death of all. Statistics will tell you asphyxiation is the most common cause of death."

"Is that so."

"It begins with feeling like there's no real emotion in your life. As though life were going on elsewhere. Then you think: If only something special would happen, a certain person paying attention to you or the like. Then you placate yourself with the idea you're no worse off than anyone else. Then you conclude that the melancholy is inevitable, and everyone else is suffering as much as you are."

"And then?"

"And then you die."

Madrid soon filled with heat, spring, and tourists. The tulips outside the Prado Museum bloomed red, and in the Botanical Garden a fuchsia bougainvillea covered an entire stone wall, which could be seen from Paseo del Prado. But, as Vicente Jiménez walked the sidewalks, the colors didn't seem as bright as in previous years. They looked faded. The food he ate for lunch seemed to lack salt, and so he added salt and more salt until every other flavor had been muted and it tasted only of salt. Certain things, for example shellfish and fruit, now seemed to have no taste at all. A certain consistency and water content, nothing more. Hard, salted potatoes with a well-done, if not charred, piece of meat was soon all that offered his taste buds any thrill at all. He presumed he was longing for an irrigation of the senses. A strong sensual experience with Jennifer. But until she paid him some more attention, he'd have to make do with what he had: Julia, books, alcohol, and himself. He read, but even reading gave him no satisfaction. In the evening he tried sitting in the room he and Julia called "the library," cognac in one hand and some old tome in the other, trying to conjure the quiet intoxication that truly good literature had always provided him. He read page after page, but his pulse held its beat, and he felt no sweetness in his blood at all. He was struck by the thought that everything he'd read in his life he'd read so he could recount it in female company. For example, Proust, the madeleine, *poof!* Why had he read that, if not to see Jennifer try to force herself inside the text, to watch her fail, sliding across its surface like a drop of water on a raincoat – and then open the door for her. Who had replaced him? Who was reading aloud to her? Which mystery was she sliding across the surface of now, which immovable iceberg was her little ice-picking brain trying to hack into? He went back to reading. Sampling Mann and Tolstoy and even Borges. When none of these authors worked, he tried Dan Brown and at least managed to concentrate for a while. Then he flipped through Julia's gossip mag, which was on the table, and when she came home they grumbled over how anyone could genuinely be interested in a rag like this. He got a text message and wished it would be from Jennifer, but it was an ad from a telephone company. When Julia went to bed he thought: The point here is to give up. Like a victim being strangled and adding to his own anxiety by fighting it. You must embrace death, you must have that courage.

The next day there was a note from Jennifer in his pigeon-hole. He read:

Last night I dreamed you were running after me. You had an enormous erection and a mad look on your face. The dream has made me feel so awful I can't come to the lecture, please leave the handouts in the library. Jennifer.

That day his lecture was mechanical, joyless. He spoke about *Paradiso*, and a few students walked out with only fifteen minutes to go. When he photocopied the illustrations by Gustave Doré, he thought they seemed exaggerated and pathetic. Paulo looked awkward with his arm around Francesca's waist, and she wasn't even radiating conviction or sensuality.

In the evening, Julia insisted he come with her to a gathering at the French embassy, but he refused. She didn't push the point. When the door shut behind her, he poured himself a cognac and sat on the sofa to watch a talk show. First there was a woman who was angry at herself because she'd dedicated her entire life to men. Then came an ad for new kitchens and panty liners, and then there was a thirty-year-old woman in a floral dress who was meeting her mother for the first time. Many people in the audience cried when they hugged each other.

At nine thirty the telephone rang. It was Inclán.

"Freshen up tomorrow," he said.

"What do you mean?"

"Freshen up. I have a solution to your problems: Beatriz."

"Where did you find her?"

"Beatriz de la Fuente. A guide at the Thyssen-Bornemisza."

"Single?"

"Yup."

"And she has nothing against a married man on his last legs?"

"She's a flower waiting for you to pluck her, Vicente."

"You and I are the flowers, Inclán. They're the hornets."

"Speak for yourself, old man. But when you show up here tomorrow, make sure you've freshened up!"

He didn't entirely trust what his colleague had said as he got dressed the next morning. But just in case, he put an extra splash of cologne on his cheeks and wore his gold Hugo Boss cuff links. Julia watched him go past, her eyebrows raised, and when he arrived at his department he thought he noticed several of the female students giving him a second look in the corridor. He knocked on Inclán's door and was let in. As he came into the room, he saw his colleague was not alone. There was a woman in one corner. She sat with her knees pressed together, wearing red high heels. He smiled at her and she smiled back. She had a beautiful face. Vicente's mouth went dry.

"Allow me to introduce you," said Inclán. "Beatriz de la Fuente. Vicente Jiménez."

They shook hands. Her hand was small, firm and smooth.

"Beatriz has been following your lectures on the *Commedia*."

"But . . . I don't understand . . . I've never seen her."

"I sit all the way at the back," the woman replied quickly. "Practically behind the pillar."

"I see. Well then. Had I known you were sitting there listening, I might have taken more care preparing my lessons."

Inclán laughed.

"May I suggest we grab a cup of coffee, the three of us. Then I'm afraid I'll have to leave you alone, because I have students to supervise."

He winked at Vicente, and they walked to the cafeteria.

A few months later Vicente Jiménez was waiting for Beatriz de la Fuente at the entrance of the Botanical Garden. They often took walks there, because Beatriz thought it was more enclosed and therefore more romantic than the large parks. There was a gentle wind; fall was on its way, and the chestnut trees around the Prado Museum were turning yellow. The traffic on Paseo del Prado was heavy, as usual. Mopeds were zipping around, filling the air with exhaust fumes and noise. Vicente felt he'd been frozen for so very long, but now he was beginning to thaw. Beatriz was a current of heat in his life. Even Jennifer had resumed her habit of sneaking notes into his pigeonhole. And this time she didn't mention any awful erections, only her regrets. He had blossomed. He was happy. He had found his Beatriz and when you find the one you need, you don't need anyone else. His pupils had darkened. Beatriz had gone to the hairdresser with him. She'd given him sunglasses as a present, and she'd helped him shop for white shirts made of stiff linen. Julia had raised her eyebrows again, said she could put two and two together, but he was looking good in any case and should be given credit for that.

"Hi."

She was standing in front of him. A wave of happiness swelled in his chest, now as every time he laid eyes on her. She was so perfect, as if tailored for him. Her short hair was combed back and dyed black. Her makeup was minimal, and she smelled of soap. She was wearing a green suede coat belted at the waist. He tried to put words to his emotions, tried saying that until now he had known nothing of female perfection. As they walked toward the secluded stone bench at the bottom of the gardens, he explained he'd always thought it was about measurable things, like the distance between the eyes and the size of the nose, the gravity of the breasts, and a number of spiritual aspects such as the intellect and sense of humor, erotic imagination, and courage. All that, one thinks women like Julia fulfill, until you get to know them and you're eaten away by boredom.

"But with you I feel alive," he said. "It's a new and unexpected feeling."

She took his hand as she listened.

"I'm angry at those words," he said. "When I say these things it sounds so banal! It's as though all the beautiful expressions have lost their gravity, and when you actually need them, when you've actually been transported to another dimension, there's no way to express yourself because the entire verbal repertoire has been turned into the hot air being spewed on talk shows!"

"But I do understand," said Beatriz.

"What is there to say when there are no words?" he said, spreading his arms wide.

"Nothing at all," she said, and spat out her gum in the goldfish pond.

They met every day. She lived in a small apartment in Argüelles, not far from the park. He took a taxi to her place at lunch, and they ate on her terrace. She often had surprises for him. Once, there were two theater tickets under his plate, another time there were tickets to a bullfight with El Juli, his favorite matador. Once, she opened the door wearing only her underwear, and on another occasion, she was swinging naked on a swing that had been installed in the middle of the living room. His libido was overflowing for tiny little her. Sometimes, they sat on her terrace, half-naked, sexes tender, drinking and sweating pleasantly in the hot night. And they talked sex. He'd never been able to talk sex with Julia. Julia didn't think sex was something you talked about, it was something you did. She didn't want to do it that often, for that matter, but that was what she'd say. And when they did do it, which was, admittedly, more often since he'd met Beatriz, it would be in the evening before they fell asleep, and in the guest room, because then they wouldn't have that cold, wet spot in the middle of the sheet, which was so unpleasant when you were trying to fall asleep. He said this to Beatriz, who pinched his nose and said it was bad form to speak ill of the people you had sex with. He felt a little mean around her. Often, he slept over at her place and in the morning, he made her coffee, went down to the bakery, and bought vanilla-filled croissants, which she ate with gusto and without mentioning her weight. Before he left, she knotted his tie, and her breath smelled of vanilla and lipstick. He thought she smelled of something else, too, hot milk maybe, or maybe it was the milkiness of her skin that encouraged the association. Maybe it was his desire to have children. He pushed it away. His train had already left the station, his children were already in the world, this wasn't worth thinking about. But if one day she did get pregnant, he would be there for her. He might even leave Julia. Maybe he would give himself the chance to begin again.

*

The Botanical Garden was as tranquil as ever. In spite of its being so central, the tourists didn't seem to venture there. He told Beatriz about the woman from his memory:

"So, I have this memory of a woman I must have known at some point. She's standing before me, naked, and writing my name on one of her breasts."

"Who is she?"

"I can't recall."

He explained that it didn't really matter who the woman was. He'd had so many. They'd been passing through him as long as he could remember, trampling on him like a doormat and pounding on him like a door. Some left things behind, a sock or a necklace. Others only an image, like this woman. But there was something about her that he couldn't shake. He wished this woman could be her, Beatriz. If only they could alter the image in his memory. Reprogram his retina. If Beatriz could be the one standing before him instead. Writing his name on one of her breasts.

"Here?" she said.

He shook his head.

"No, not here. Somewhere else. Wherever you want. Wherever you won't be cold."

He looked down at the ground, ashamed at the silly suggestion.

"But isn't here as good as anywhere else?"

She takes off her clothes. He is laughing incredulously, but she is serious. She wades out into the pond with the water lilies. When the water is up to her knees, she asks him to throw her a pen. She is standing there – like the woman in his memory, but more beautiful.

"Perfect," he says.

61

She writes slowly. There's a gust of wind. He thinks: It's all too beautiful to be true, and suddenly, out of nowhere, Inclán enters the picture. He puts his jacket on a branch, places his shoes on the strip of sand, and wades out to Beatriz. He embraces her, and when she looks up, he kisses her.

"Darling," he says. "What are you doing standing naked in the middle of the pond?"

As Jerónimo begins to explain, he blacks out.

"We have to find somewhere to sit," he says, putting one arm around Vicente and the other around Beatriz.

There are of course thousands of explanations. He knows they're coming, and he plans on listening, in spite of the dizziness and nausea. They're civilized people. They won't end up in a verbal tussle, are even less likely to end up in a physical one. They sit by a rusty iron table, and Inclán searches his pockets for a pack of cigarettes. Beatriz is still naked, though Vicente has said the image is long ruined and she should get dressed now. Her breasts droop toward the table, and they bear his name, though the last letter is missing – the pen must have slipped when Inclán arrived, because the "t" ends in a downward curving line, heading toward her belly button. Her eyes dart.

"I understand that you're upset," says Inclán. "But I only meant well. We only meant well. You were asphyxiating. Beatriz wanted an adventure, our sex life had stalled somewhat, and I thought . . . it would be good if it were you, and no one else. Let's say I gave you 'artificial respiration,' and Beatriz the opportunity to dine on something out of the ordinary. And anyway, her name isn't Beatriz. We made that up just to fit in your Dante world. She's called Raimunda."

Raimunda shrugs and looks remorseful.

He doesn't vomit. Nor does he hit Inclán in the face. He just sits there, fidgeting, as though he had a stomachache, though he doesn't. When, finally, he gets up and leaves the two of them at the iron table, he feels no self-pity at all, in fact he recognizes the feeling of being left by Beatriz. It had worried him in each happy moment. Now he's living what he had fearfully imagined so many times before. He gets up from the table, reaches out a hand, and takes his leave of Raimunda and Inclán, then walks with his head held high toward the exit. Julia calls, asks if he wants to join her for a cocktail, and he says no. Then Julia says she can't talk for long because she's about to try on a dress, but he can call her if he changes his mind. He walks down Paseo del Prado. The people around him look happy, but he knows the smiles are fake, and that everyone was dying this same death.

CIRCE

If you take the bus from Plaza Castilla, get off at the construction site for the new El Corte Inglés, and then trudge a few hundred meters through the mud, you'll find a gypsy woman with eight kids and a crystal ball. If you have a few euros to spare, you can find out all sorts of things. It was Gaia who knew where she lived and we braved the muck during our lunch break. It was cold and you had to cover your ears so they wouldn't chafe or whatever.

"Does he love me as much as I love him?" Gaia said, and the old lady looked into the ball.

"Yes. He does," she said.

I wondered what to ask when it was my turn. Gaia had the good questions, not me. I mostly wanted to know what was for dinner, how big my boobs would get, and if my hair had that Mariah Carey thing where it just kept growing. But luck wasn't on my side because one of the lady's babies woke up. She stuck a sprig of rosemary between Gaia's boobs and then the curtain fell right in front of our faces. It smelled like smoke and something else, maybe boiled chicken.

That visit was right after Gaia had had her surgery, and I was about to start ninth grade. Mom had a new job and couldn't take us to or from school anymore. Jaime was growing up, hair had sprouted on his chin, and he'd gotten gross, like boys do. Once a week, Raquel, a lady from Ecuador, came over to clean and do the ironing. "You have no idea how hard I have to work to afford you," Mom would say to Raquel.

Gaia would pose in front of the mirror, admiring her new boobs. Jaime would fish out boogers. One time when lunch was over, Gaia said she could take me back to school, since she was going that way anyway.

On the walls at school were pictures of angels, and the brushstrokes were like the ones in a painting I'd seen where someone with a really big mouth was screaming. I asked Gaia what she thought about them. She said I should make sure the boys were respectful. Not let them talk more than us girls did and stuff like that. Then she said she and her boyfriend, who was at least twenty-five, had put her money in a high-risk fund in Russia and that she'd earned five grand in one night.

"If you have any money, I can give it to him," she said. "Maybe you could get new boobs, too."

"Why?" I asked.

"Because they're small."

"Eh. They probably haven't finished growing yet," I said.

"Your call," Gaia said with a shrug.

We kept walking.

"So, what do you do with them?" I asked.

"With what?"

"Your boobs."

"Don't be stupid. Baby."

"Like, I don't even have a boyfriend."

"Well, of course not. You don't have any boobs."

We arrived at school.

"And you," said Gaia. "Remember what I said. Make sure you make your own decisions, OK? Like my boyfriend says: Stand your ground, or someone will stand in your place."

She blew a bubble. It popped and stuck to her nose.

"Ciao," she said and left.

Gaia was the new Gaia now. The new Gaia with her new boobs. I was still the same old me, even though I was the youngest. Same old thirteen-year-old Encarna with her same old boobs. But, like, high-risk funds in Russia, I mean, I didn't even have a boyfriend so who would even care.

"Money," Mom said at the dinner table. "I hate money."

"Why?" Jaime asked.

"Because it's so damn dirty," said Mom. "Who knows who's touched it. At the checkout, all you do is handle it. Put it in small compartments and stuff it into tubes that go to some sort of money depot under the store. And if you scratch your nose before washing your hands, it's curtains for you. Infection time."

"What about fruit?" Jaime said. "Who knows about *that*. Somebody could've masturbated with the apple you're eating."

There was a long pause. Then Gaia said:

"Jaime, have you ever masturbated with an apple?"

He replied by shoving his index finger up his nose. Gaia looked thoughtful, and those high-risk funds popped into my head.

"Let's be clear about one thing," said Gaia as she changed into her pajamas. "There's nothing more fun than sex."

"How many times have you done it?" I asked.

"I've lost count," said Gaia.

"How was it?"

"Really fucking good. Amazing. The only thing that's worth the pains."

"Which pains?"

"Life, the struggle, hell – everything. There's only one thing that balances out all the shit, and that's sex."

In school the next day the teacher said we had to think about our futures. He said there was a stand with brochures in the hallway, and you could have a poke around to help you decide what to be when you grew up. If you're lucky the guidance counselor will pass by, he said, and then you can have a talk with her, because if there was anyone who knew about those things, it was her, after all she'd studied it for several years. The brochures were in alphabetical order. "Builder," I could see clearly. "Assistant," too. "Doctor" was also an option. Otherwise it was mostly the carpets I was seeing, cos they were pretty filthy. Somebody needed to give them a good vacuum. The striplights flickered and that meant they were almost dead. And the boys behaved. No one said anything stupid, even though I was ready for it.

And then she showed up, the guidance counselor. And it was just me standing there, so when she unlocked the door to her office she waved me right in. Next to her was a potted cactus. Behind her, out the window, was the gloomy schoolyard.

"How's your sister keeping?" she asked.

"She has new boobs."

The basketball net moved in the wind. The trees were bare, and the guidance counselor was wearing salmon-colored lip gloss and had straight yellow teeth. It was silent, except for the fans, which you could hear whirring in the guidance counselor's office, the halls, the classrooms, and everywhere else in school.

"Is that so. New boobs. There you have it."

She riffled through some papers on the desk. Her heel scraped the floor.

"All right. And what does this young lady want to do with her life?"

"It's not that easy."

"Dream. Wish. You're young."

"I can't think of anything fun."

I was mostly thinking about *Julius Caesar* when I said that. About how it was no fun taking notes while someone else was talking and how someone had said, the teacher maybe, that note-taking was a must if you wanted to get anywhere in this world. When I took notes I did it to practice my handwriting, so that all the love letters I'd write when I got a lover would look beautiful. And I thought about home economics, how woolen sweaters had to soak in fabric softener for two minutes before being rolled up in towels. Otherwise they'd never dry, and wool wasn't something you could hang over the heater or in the airing cupboard. And equations. Somebody told me I didn't understand them because they were too simple. You didn't know what X was. But if you didn't know, how was I supposed to know? It was really rare for me to know something that no one else knew, except for that thing about Gaia. And then there was biology, of course, dissecting worms that were pinned in place and sliced down the middle. Not for me.

"But you must like something? There must be something that's fun?"

I thought about English. Our teacher had one of those toupees, and one time it blew off during a handball tournament he'd insisted on playing in. He was basically just kinda gross, and the English book was a harsh orange color. No, English was not for me. Physics could be my thing, smoke and Bunsen burners were fun, but I'd heard there was a lot of math when it got advanced so I think I'll skip that too, I said to the guidance counselor.

She looked me in the eyes. She put her hand on my shoulder.

"But sweetie, there must be something you think is fun?"

"I can't think of anything."

"Nothing?"

"Maybe high-risk funds in Russia."

"Building your future on high-risk funds in Russia might not be wise."

"Then I don't know."

She looked through some papers. Maybe they were comments from teachers, maybe it was a manual for how to get young people to choose a high school.

She threw open her arms and smiled.

"There must be something you like!"

She seemed unnaturally happy. As if something funny had occurred to her, beyond me and beyond the room we were in. Maybe she was thinking of her lover.

"I can't think of anything," I snapped.

"All children like something."

I remembered what Gaia had said. She was my sister, so there was a chance I'd like what she liked.

"Yeah," I said. "Sex is pretty fun. I could imagine working in sex."

The guidance counselor's leg gave a little push and the chair rolled backwards. She looked at her papers and outside, behind her, the wind rattled the backboard. You were supposed to hit the red square with the ball. And if you hit it right in the middle and not too hard, you could almost be sure you'd score.

"Excuse me a moment," she said.

After a while she returned with the school nurse. The school nurse asked me to follow her to her office, and I said goodbye to the guidance counselor, who shut the door behind us. I was handed a cup of tea and I added three sugar cubes, which left a syrupy gunk at the bottom.

"So, tell me about your experiences," the school nurse said.

"Experiences?"

"Yes. About what you just told Maruja. That's terrible. You're so young."

"Hey," I said. "I'm not that much younger than anyone else."

After the nine thirty break, the principal was roped in. His desk was made of a reddish wood and through the window behind him you could see the cars in the parking lot. The principal's car was in the middle of it and was red, maybe he'd let his wife pick it out.

"Did your wife pick out the car?" I asked.

"I don't have a wife. I'm newly divorced," he said.

"Did your ex-wife pick out the car?"

"Yes," he said and sighed.

Then he said that in life, you must have goals. Fight and get ahead. Short-term and long-term goals. You have to fight, the fight was what was important.

"But it's just all so boring. Taking notes and stuff," I said.

"That's the path you have to take. Don't you under-stand? It's like a highway. Imagine Madrid, and imagine Alicante. It's impossible to get to Alicante if you don't take the highway. It's impossible to get to the ocean without crossing the scorched terrain of La Mancha."

He looked pleased with himself for having said that.

"There has to be another way," I said. "Other fun things to do."

He looked at me.

"What do you mean?"

"Other fun things. Like sex."

He looked out at the parking lot, but it was too late. I'd seen that spark in his eyes. Gaia had talked about how something sparked in old men's eyes when they wanted it.

"Of course sex can be work," I said and sat up straight in the chair. "You just have to find someone who wants to buy it. Demand and stuff, you know."

I got perks. The physics teacher set up a special table for me to do fun experiments, made me the boss of the station. The others had labs about kinetic energy, while I was putting lithium in glasses of water. Cleaning up took forever, and by the time chemistry class started, I was still putting away the Bunsen burners in the closet with the skeleton in it, so I got out of writing organic formulas.

We go to the old gypsy lady sometimes, me and Gaia. Her children walk barefoot through the muck, and once she said that life always ends in tears, so you had to get some laughs in before you die, because then you've won. Once she said we were dumb for thinking we were going to be happy. You can't choose what kind of happy you're going to be, only the kind of unhappy, and that's good enough.

ODETTE KLOCKARE

When the removal van drove into our village that spring, Malcolm was still one of us. We sat in Magdalena's kitchen and watched the truck park in front of the small white house on the hill. Three men carried in boxes, and Magdalena ran the coffee machine not once but twice before they were done. By then, we'd seen the polished mahogany furniture carried up the stone steps and into the darkness beyond the open door. Then came the plastic-wrapped hangers, the floor lamps, the piano, and finally the candlesticks with crystal droplets, waving and glinting in the afternoon light like frozen tears. No one said anything at Magdalena's kitchen table when the removal van drove away. We could see no change: no curtains being hung, no one walking around the living room arranging furniture or decorating. The house was as it had been for the past half year: still and silent.

"She's called Odette Klockare," Magdalena said.

"She's up there," said Malcolm.

We looked at the top-floor window, but saw nothing. Malcolm swore she was standing there – she was smoking and looking down at us. We swore there was nothing there, except for an old window in need of renovation, and what a crying shame it was that the previous owners had let it go to rack and ruin.

The next day, Magdalena ran into her by the mailboxes. She was wearing a long black robe.

"It's a long way to the city from here," Magdalena said.

"What do I care about the city?" Odette Klockare replied.

"All I said was it's a long way to the city," Magdalena repeated.

Spring arrived early. The birch trees had bloomed at the start of April, and by May the water was already warm. In the evening we floated in the lake, carried along by the surface currents, occasionally reaching our feet down into the cold underneath. Some of us jumped from the tower, some rowed out and went fishing, some sold ice cream from the kiosk. Malcolm, he stretched out on a pool lounger under the beech trees, which were growing in the wrong direction because they'd confused the light bouncing off the water with the light from the sky. Everything in his life was static, pleasant, and mild. He was twenty-nine years old, was nobody and had nothing. Only the piano – he let himself pound and caress that.

"Considering how things are now," he'd say, "the idea that my house will one day be full of screaming children and all the other family racket seems pretty awful."

And on one of those evenings, after Odette Klockare had settled into her house and when Malcolm was on the pool lounger looking up at the leaves, she appeared on the beach, walked up to Malcolm, and said she wanted to speak with him. She stood in front of us on the grass, and under her matte, milky skin, her long legs appeared shriveled. Her shoulders were slender and stooped, curved like a spoon around those old breasts. Her feet were turned out like a dancer's, and her hair was twisted into a low bun.

"Go ahead," Malcolm said.

"Not here," Odette said and looked at us.

"Go ahead," Malcolm repeated. "There are no secrets in this village."

Odette put down her bag.

"I've heard you play the piano," she said.

"Yes," he replied.

"I need someone to teach me."

When he didn't reply, she added:

"Someone who can give me lessons."

It was a shame the evening sun was in our eyes and we couldn't see her expression.

"And where would we do that?" he said.

"At my house," she replied.

Malcolm didn't know what to say; maybe that's why he nodded. He thought he could cancel later on, during the week. Stop by some night, knock and say he'd gotten in over his head.

"Can we begin tomorrow?" she asked. "Seven o'clock."

"I have to check the calendar," Malcolm said.

"Do call if you can't," she replied. "Otherwise I'll be expecting you."

She'd already picked up her bag and was on her way when she said that last bit. She didn't look back, not at Malcolm or any of the rest of us.

That same night, when we ran into him by the church during our evening walk, Malcolm said he was going to cancel on Odette Klockare – she'd surprised him with her question, after all. He was going to insist they reschedule.

"Yes," we said, "though isn't this an excellent opportunity to find out more about her?"

We deliberated. People are blank canvases when they arrive in our village. Who knows what's behind them, what they've done, who they are. A home can tell you. Framed photos, smells from the refrigerator, trash cans. What's being grown in the garden, how the living room is furnished. Whether the milk curdled in the coffee, when the place was last aired out.

Malcolm said OK, for our sake, for the sake of the village, he would visit her once.

He rang her doorbell at seven the next night. She opened up, and he stepped into the hall. The blue of her eyes struck him first. They were like fish eyes: no depth to them at all, and watery.

"Come in," she said.

The house smelled of coffee, camphor, and smoke. Thick red rugs were spread on the dark floor. The wallpaper was old and had red velvet flocking. There were several ashtrays out, and in one was a cigarette in a holder, smoldering. The piano was in the middle of the living room. She'd lifted the cover, and when he came close he realized she must have scrubbed it before his arrival, because it had a whiff of ammonia. She carried over one of the dining-room chairs and sat. Malcolm took hold of her fingers, which seemed so old, brittle, and dry that they might crumble if he squeezed too hard.

"I've always dreamed of this," she said when her fingers were on the keys.

"It's a lot of work," Malcolm said.

"I know," she said. "But nonetheless, I've always dreamed of this."

There was something in her tone that moved him, something ragged and hoarse, as though this were the first time in a long time that she'd spoken of her dreams with anyone, or that she'd spoken with anyone at all.

Teaching an old lady to play was as he thought it would be: difficult. Not only were her hands stubborn and stiff, they were far too small to assert any control over the keys. But Malcolm was a proud man, and a commitment was a commitment and nothing to sniff at. A lesson was forty minutes long. You couldn't leave after half an hour.

Forty minutes passed, and he got up to leave.

"Can't you stay for a moment?" Odette wondered aloud. "Have a cognac with me? It's so empty here in the evenings."

She went to the kitchen, leaving him alone in the living room. He looked around for photos, but there was only one, of Odette Klockare herself. She was younger. She was wearing a pink felt hat and laughing so the top row of her teeth was visible. She had beautiful straight teeth, and the hair sticking out from her hat was flaxen. Maybe she wasn't as old as he'd thought. She'd always had white hair. He searched for anything else that might be of interest. He looked out into the garden. Roses were blooming. Red, yellow, pink, white. Beyond the rosebushes you could see the fields. The sky was large and beautiful. Outside the terrace doors was a small wooden chair. That's where she sits, Malcolm thought. That's where she sits in the evenings when she's all alone.

Odette came into the living room. They drank some cognac, then they stood there. Silent and tense.

"See you next Monday then," she said after a while.

"Yes," he replied and left.

*

A week passed. Each day when Malcolm woke up he thought: Today I'm going over to Odette Klockare's to tell her I won't be coming back. All of Tuesday and Wednesday it rained and he stayed indoors, lit a fire, and listened to the pattering on the roof, unable to make up his mind to put on a raincoat and go outside.

On Thursday there was a dinner at Mona and Bertil's, and Bertil said on Wednesday he'd seen Odette Klockare on the bus to Lund. She'd looked happy, he said. It was strange to see a smile on that face, he added. She had one of those unsmiling faces, so it was difficult to imagine her smile as anything other than a crooked grin. But she'd been truly beautiful sitting there on the bus, smiling, he said, his eyebrows raised in surprise. Magdalena muttered that she'd run into Odette by the mailboxes that morning and the woman was as grumpy as ever, barely a hello and no comment on the weather, either.

Sunday arrived, and Malcolm thought once again: I must go over there and tell her there will be no more piano-playing. He told us this when we met by the church after our evening walk, said he was feeling terrible. Maybe she'd gone around all week looking forward to it. Maybe she'd practiced. Maybe it was because of him that she was smiling on the bus. He could go one last time. Give her one more lesson and recommend another place where she could learn. Or a book. Teaching yourself to play – lots of people did that.

"But then again," Malcolm said, "her loneliness is so heartrending, it makes you want to help her."

We replied that yes, indeed, Odette Klockare was lonely, but loneliness is something you have to bear because everyone is lonely in some way. That's just the way it is, and Malcolm couldn't save Odette from hers, or us from ours, or even himself from his own.

The second lesson was like the first. They sat there and her hands were unyielding and hard. The piano would not be persuaded. Malcolm's impatience must have been apparent, because suddenly she seemed sad and said that trying to learn the piano at her age was a foolish idea.

"You can't teach an old dog new tricks," she said. "And clearly, neither can you teach old ladies to play."

"Let's take a break," Malcolm said.

"But I'm not completely worthless, you know," she said. "I can write poetry."

She disappeared up the stairs and quickly returned with some papers.

"Here," she said, handing them over.

There were three long poems written in a meter he didn't know, but he could see they were well written. He read them and looked up at her. Reading and then smiling, telling her how good they were. He was the first to see them, she said. These specific poems only he had read. There was a bond between them now. A secret only they shared, a secret that was the start of something forbidden, because nothing unites people like a secret, and nothing is as forbidden. But in spite of the secret, Malcolm spent the following week deliberating over whether he should continue the lessons, especially when he was having coffee with us in Magdalena's kitchen and saw Odette walking around her house across the way. In those moments, she was like a stranger to him, and when he talked about her we still thought he was being unguarded and honest, which increased our solidarity as well as our knowledge of Odette.

But he didn't mention her poems then. He knew how pathetic it would sound to us. Pretentious, frivolous. He didn't mention them because he didn't want us to make fun of her – he no longer trusted us, was beginning to see us as strangers and her as a friend. Soon he stopped deliberating over the lessons. He looked forward to Monday nights. He felt happy when he passed by her house.

Around this point in the story it's harder to get a grip on what actually happened. When you bumped into him on a walk or sat with him in Magdalena's kitchen, he was reticent. His eyes darted, he rolled crumbs between his fingertips and rattled his spoon in his cup even after the coffee was gone. And we said to him:

"We all have our stuff. None of us are angels – all of us have baggage that's unpleasant to unpack."

Then he'd hold up his hands and say:

"OK, OK. I'll tell you."

The first time he touched Odette, it was out of sympathy. He'd been sitting next to her on the piano stool, holding those bird-hands of hers and trying in vain to get them to pound the keys with conviction. He'd played a piece himself and shown her the force needed to dominate the instrument. He'd hit the keys hard, harder than the piece demanded. Odette had slumped at his side, and the candlestick crystals had quivered. He was angry: the woman couldn't learn, had no musical talent whatsoever, and it was ridiculous for her to have gone out and bought a piano, like some object that would make her seem refined. And she must have noticed his irritation, because she burst into tears. Sat on the chair, hiding her face in her hands. Those small bird-shoulders shaking.

"Listen," he said, reaching out his hand. "Take it easy. Everyone is good at something. Maybe music just isn't your thing."

She leaned against his shoulder. His anger faded. He thought: I've never been this close to a woman. He stroked her hair. Then her earlobe. It was so smooth. Gripped by a sudden curiosity, he wanted to know if her neck was as smooth. He stuck one finger inside the collar of her blouse and touched the skin there. It was. Then she turned to him, took his hands, and pressed her mouth to his. She tasted salty from the tears wetting her face. First it felt as though the blood had frozen in his veins. Odette Klockare's tongue in his mouth, her salt inside him! Old age entering him – he who still had his youth. He wanted to push her away and go home, now with an excellent excuse to end the lessons. But he had another idea, a somewhat wily one. During the seconds they spent kissing, the thought arose that this could get him out of his predicament. In a few hours, he would be able to remedy his inexperience. Perhaps not with his dream woman, but no matter. Compassion, which had led him to touch her in the first place, had become calculation. And that calculation led to the sound of Odette's sheets as they lay on the bed, and the coolness of her hands as they feebly gripped the back of his neck. A whiff of moth repellent from the mattress blended with her dry perfume. Her body was motionless, and in certain moments he thought she might be asleep. He wondered if she were aware that it was him she was making love with, or if she was thinking of something else, someone else. He also thought: What difference does it make?

*

They continued to meet on Mondays, the weekly lesson their excuse. He would arrive at hers at seven, and they'd go up to the bedroom, where they'd take off their clothes and get under her covers. They didn't always make love; sometimes they'd just lie there, holding each other, listening to the ravens and the magpies hopping off and onto the crown of the chimney above. Odette would light a candle and turn off the lights. On certain evenings during the winter months, the force of the wind made the entire house creak. And they'd say this was what being a person should be like. You should be snuggled up together in a warm place while the wind rampaged outside. This was what the whole human experience was about, and it was pain-free moments like these that enabled you to be happy. It was as good as it got, they told each other.

At first, he was afraid that Odette would make demands. Want to meet more often. Want him to stay longer. At her age, perhaps it was natural to think that a relationship implied commitment. But soon he breathed a sigh of relief, for Odette made no demands at all. Sometimes as he was leaving, she'd say she was going to read or work on a poem, and she'd say this with such joy that he knew she was relieved to see him go. He relaxed. Their encounters continued through the winter. Once a week, one hour. The weeks took on an inner rhythm: Sundays were long and full of anticipation, Tuesdays were long and torturous, because the next Monday was as distant as it could be. He began to doubt that Odette felt the same way. He'd feel jealous just thinking of her waking up, wrapping herself in that black robe, lighting a cigarette, and going to the mailbox to pick up a newspaper, maybe trading a quip with Magdalena, only to go back home and put on the coffee, heat the milk, toast a few slices of white bread, which she ate with butter and bitter orange marmalade. Perhaps she would look out across the plains and enjoy the silence and the hot coffee, thinking lovemaking was all well and good, but how nice that no one was there, insisting on sharing her breakfast. He no longer thought of her as old. To him, her age was just an unfortunate garment she happened to be dressed in – under it she was young. He told us he could see her true self, just as she was. And he said it with such conviction that we did in fact believe it to be true.

He arrived one Monday evening to find her in particularly good spirits. She'd made soup and laid out a picnic on the rug in the bedroom, along with tall, slender-stemmed wine glasses and burning candles. They'd never eaten together before that night, and until now he'd assumed the cognac glasses they always drank from were the only ones she had.

"I have to tell you," said Odette. "I've met some fantastic people."

She talked about a group she'd been going to, where everyone had one thing in common: they'd been touched by the divine. He laughed when she said it.

"Odette," he said. "Are you all right?"

"It's true," she said when he'd finished laughing. "I understand this might sound strange, but it's true."

He said the soup was delicious, as was the wine, but maybe it was time to move to the bed. Turn off the lights and lie there, listening to the wind.

"Perhaps we should finish talking about this first," she replied with a hint of authority.

She talked about how she'd been taking part in the group for almost two months now, but hadn't wanted to mention it because she didn't want him to think she was crazy. But now she was so sure, so fulfilled by the meetings, that she no longer had any doubt: Jesus was the best, most incredible thing that had ever happened.

"He's rock 'n' roll," she said. "No one has ever been more rock 'n' roll."

He wasn't laughing anymore. He'd let the wine go to his head, making him anticipate all the lovely things that were about to take place between her sheets. But now he felt it sinking to his toes and settling there like cold lead.

"But Odette," he said. "You can't do this."

"Come with me," she said. "We can share the experience."

"Forget about it," he said. "You can just forget about it."

"OK," Odette said.

Despite his aversion to the sort of gathering Odette was describing, he felt wounded by how little she'd insisted. Had she insisted, it would've been proof of her affection. Of her wanting him at her side for this nuttery. She could have insisted for the sake of it. Now it was clear she could carry on just as well without him. Maybe there was a man her age there, he thought. Someone who could make love as old men do.

He tried to talk some sense into her, convince her that these people were just meddling with people who spent too much time at home alone. They were taking advantage of her and her loneliness. They were experts at that. If it would make Odette feel better, they could have two "piano lessons" a week instead of one. That wouldn't raise an eyebrow. Then she'd be less alone. But Odette shook her head.

"I'm going again tomorrow," she said.

"Don't I mean anything to you anymore?" he asked.

He stood up with the intention of going home. She stayed on the floor in front of him. Looked up at him with something unpleasant and shiny in her eyes. Infected, he thought. Odette Klockare has gone and gotten infected. I can't be with this woman anymore.

He went home to his little house, and it was as cold as usual.

Well, yes. Sure, we can remember Odette's salvation. It coincided with the snails and the heat, didn't it, but it was the kind of unpleasant thing we'd probably have noticed anyway. That old maid up on the hill had one foot in the grave. Well, when the devil gets old, even he turns to God. People let their dogs shit outside her house and someone had left a wad of tobacco-stained spit in the middle of her driveway. No, we hadn't behaved like God's favorite children, but then again, she was the one who came to our village, started taking piano lessons from Malcolm, and then went and got saved. Magdalena could tell you all about the dopey smile on Odette's face when they ran into each other by the mailboxes each morning.

"First I thought she was difficult because she was grumpy. But now I know she's a damn sight better when she's a grump than when she's happy."

And it was around then that we villagers began to suspect something wasn't right about those Monday evenings at Odette's. While everyone else was out on the streets collecting snails, her house was silent, dead. And those of us snail-picking couldn't hear any keys being tinkled at all, even though the window was open. Not to mention we'd all agreed to go out picking at the same time. We crept a little closer. We cupped our ears. Put our hands around our eyes and peered through the living room and saw that the piano was shut. We went round the back of the house. There was a ladder. Some of us climbed up, others had to satisfy themselves with cupping their ears.

And there they were.

"If only you two hadn't been so naked," we said to him when we saw him by the church that same night. "You were going at it like a couple of rabbits. Never mind her age or her salvation."

We asked him to understand our surprise, so we could understand his shame. We said it was in the nature of shame to deny and deflect, but shame could be seen as a purification process – embrace it and let it heal you. We just wanted him to confess. And we wanted him to acknowledge that in what we had witnessed there had been no tenderness at all. It was the deceit that concerned us. The sham humanity, when we all knew that right then, both he and she were no more than two animals. We reached out our hands. As if to say: Lay yourself down. Accept your inferiority and receive our forgiveness. Then everything can go back to normal.

He went his way, and it would be another six months before we saw him again. Then he came over, one unremarkable night. He fed us each a spoonful of his venom in Magdalena's kitchen. After some small talk, he said he was struck by how ugly we were. The disorder around us. All the dirty cups and the TV in the background, the chirpy female voice, the volume doubling when the ads came on. He pointed at the refrigerator. Our eating habits. Bruised-looking, plastic-wrapped sausages. Couldn't we have taken a look at ourselves, instead of leeching on to Odette's windowsill?

He stood at the window and looked over at Odette's. The house had sunk into itself since they'd stopped seeing each other. The paint had begun flaking, and she never showed her face on the street anymore. Odette: who would live and die here and then be buried in a grave on the far side of the graveyard, where the grass is taller and the wind pummels the slope in the winter, for there lie those who were not born in the village but merely spent their lives here. That's how it is, and that's how it has always been – we reached for Malcolm, who took a step back.

"Malcolm," we said.

Magdalena put on the coffee. Washed the filthy cups. Mona stretched.

"Malcolm," she whispered.

But it was too late, he'd already walked out the door. We saw him cross the road and knock. He waited. We waited. Finally, the door opened.

"Come now," we heard him say.

They stood at the bus stop by the mailboxes. Two shadowy, slim figures, their breath clouding as they spoke. They stamped their feet, leaned against each other now and then and looked at each other, but we couldn't see their faces – they'd wrapped their scarves around their heads and only their eyes peered out. The Lund bus arrived, stopped, gobbled them up, and drove out of our village.

The percolator gurgled. The house across the way was empty, and its soulless windows stared into the dark.

AND BY THE ELEVATOR HUNG A KEY

All of my dreams fit inside that apartment: the view across the palms in the Viveros Gardens to the Carmelite convent's towers and the minarets inside the city walls; the scent of wet earth and the sea. I thought about Teresa's place, her hallway with its black, bird-patterned wallpaper, which looked salt-encrusted in the light. Down Teresa's hall was her kitchen, with its spices in small bags. She bought the spices at the market, and when she cooked they fell to the floor in uneven piles. You ended up stepping in them and scenting the soles of your feet.

The real estate agent had said:

"What with the zoo down there, the smell from the animals, you might be able to get a discount if you make up your mind right now."

On the nights the flying cockroaches found their way up onto the balcony railing, we would close the doors and windows. We'd lie beneath the bedroom fan, which, spin by spin, cut the silence into fragments, sad fragments, or perhaps they were no longer that sad.

An enervating heat, May in Valencia. At the convenience store, I bought a bottle of wine, which I drank on the balcony, looking out over the view of the palms and the convent's blue dome in the sunlight. I heard my neighbors arguing as they cleaned. I went up to ask them to be quiet, lingered outside the door for a while, listening to their voices. Then I went back downstairs and took in the view, thinking how lonely an apartment this big was, that I should probably go down to the zoo one of these days.

Admission was five euros. I was asked to take care when crossing the crocodile bridge because it was due to be fixed. I stopped in front of the hippopotamus, whose cage (or pen?) was just big enough for her to turn around in. It was the same for the white tiger and the rhinoceros. I didn't notice the gorillas that visit. I went home and made inquiries. The zoo was temporary, and had been since 1958. The space "is the only thing that can occasion complaint, for the hygiene is exemplary: the cages are all fumigated at least five times per year, and vermin are rare." I wrote a few lines about this, and they were published in one of the daily papers. After a few weeks, I found a job stamping documents at customs and shelved the zoo polemic. The only time I thought about it was when I walked to the tram in the mornings: there would surely have been fewer dead cockroaches on the sidewalk if the zoo hadn't been so close by. Otherwise, those mornings were cool, with a ripple of salt from the sea. The air felt clean, and people weren't really on the go yet.

When Teresa came over, we'd sit on the balcony during the day, closing the doors at nightfall and lying down beneath the fan. We often heard the neighbors cleaning and moving cabinets, sometimes fighting.

Teresa would sing: *Così è l'amore che viene e va, gioie e dolori sempre ti dà*, convinced it was an old Roman song with some kind of immeasurable wisdom. I'd laugh. One afternoon, she took a cotton swab, dipped it in perfume, cleaned her belly button, and said: "It's about time."

"Maybe we should go up there and get to know them," I said.

And so we did. Teresa bought a bottle of pink liqueur, and I bought black tulips from the flower shop by the Carmelite convent. Then, that evening, we went up to the neighbors, Teresa still smelling of the perfume in her belly button.

The man was in a wheelchair and was brittle and withered like an old leaf. The woman was also brittle and withered like an old leaf, but she wasn't in a wheelchair. She walked around the apartment with a dustcloth flopping like a dog's ear from her apron pocket, wiping the glossy cherrywood furniture. She put our tulips between two red geraniums and said the cockroaches were multiplying and it was the zoo's fault, it was so close by and with everything warming up in general, the air was spreading E. coli particles, bringing them up to her balcony with the slightest breeze – that explained the cockroaches.

"They should shut it down," she said. "So many animals. So close to us people."

"I worry about the gorillas most," said the man. "The male. I'd never seen a sad animal before him. You can't get over that gorilla's eyes."

"Always so melodramatic," the woman said. "A gorilla is a gorilla. Maybe they can be sad in a gorilla way, but they can't cry."

"They can," the man said, and looked out the window.

The woman ran the cloth over the table, around the pink bottle and Teresa's key ring.

"You hear that? He's on his way out. I barely have it in me to care for him anymore."

She lowered her voice.

"But he's been given a place at the nursing home. That'll be his next stop – finally, after all these years!"

She put her index finger to her lips and smothered the end of the sentence, which had come out like a muffled cry.

We stayed a little while longer. They told us their names were Antonio and Inés. Teresa helped herself to the liqueur. Our black tulips looked dirty between those red geraniums. We told them about the bird wallpaper we'd just put up in my hallway, identical to Teresa's, and the woman seemed suspicious. Teresa sang the Roman song about love coming and going, and the old lady said she didn't understand Italian and had never liked Italians, they put on airs. Once, on holiday in Rimini, she'd been woken up by some old-timer under her window shouting about tomatoes for sale. That would never happen in Spain, she said, here everything is orderly because it's part of the national tradition. Not that she wanted to bring up the Catholic kings, but if you didn't get a hold on a country's character from the get-go, the battle was lost.

Eventually, a drawn-out snore came from the wheelchair. We got up, took our leave of the woman, and made for the door, saying it had been lovely but time was marching on.

The summer became stifling. We lay on Malvarrosa Beach during the day and sat on the balcony at night. Often the air was still; if there was a breeze at all, it smelled of pigeon droppings and dirty straw. Inés and Antonio continued to fight with the window open, and at ten each night their daughter would call from Madrid. Once, they talked about going on vacation, but Inés said when it came to hotels you couldn't trust the quality of the cleaning or the food. And anyway, home is where the heart is, so why bother.

They picked Antonio up in September. Two carers dressed in white helped carry the wheelchair down the stairs, and Teresa and I took turns peering through the peephole in my door. It looked like he was asleep in his chair.

"She's probably drugged him," Teresa said.

He was packed off in a yellow car that bore the words *La Santa Hermandad de la Virgen*. We stood on the balcony and watched them drive off. Upstairs, Inés was pottering around in the apartment, and in the afternoon, we saw her come home with a yellow canary in a cage. Soon we could hear it on her balcony. We heard her, too: she whistled, sang, pushed around the furniture. In the evenings we heard glasses clattering, and Teresa said she'd bet the woman was drinking what was left of the pink liqueur. Teresa put a record on, and soon the old lady banged on the floor. I turned it down.

"We have to go visit that old man," Teresa said. "I know where La Santa Hermandad is, we can take the bus tomorrow."

We visited him the next day. We told the nuns we were his grandchildren and watched them serve him colorless liquids, which he drank through a straw. The nuns were stern, and they moved furniture around, too, made sure things were dusted, that the skirting boards at least had a cloth run across them. By the elevator hung a key. To get out of the home, you had to be able to stick it in the lock straight and give it a half turn, then you'd hear the elevator start up. You had to wonder if some old person had tried to jimmy it into the hole at some point. You had to wonder if Antonio had noticed it. Old, withered hands that must have been shaking, unable to hit the mark.

"It must be frustrating not to be dealt an honorable death," Teresa said. "To be poisoned by gruel."

"Eh," Antonio said.

"Just you wait," Teresa said. "You'll be dead in a week."

"I can only dream."

The nuns brought apple liqueur on a tray for me and Teresa. Medicine for the old man.

"It was nice of you to visit," he said. "How's Inés doing?"

"She's bought a canary," I said.

"I suspected she would."

A nun put pills on his tongue, and he swallowed them with water. Manolo Escobar was singing on the radio on the other side of the room. Teresa asked where Antonio's bedroom was, and we went there. She took a mosquito net out of her bag and fixed it over the window, so it would shield against other animals, too. Antonio said he'd gotten a few bites, and Teresa dressed them with the disinfectant from the bathroom cabinet. There was a hand cream in there too, and Teresa guessed it had been for a while, because it smelled stale.

Antonio was asleep in his wheelchair when we left. When we got home, we went up to Inés to say hello from her husband. She said it was good of us to visit him – he was probably sitting around all alone – and she'd go over there herself one day, when she had the time. On the balcony, the yellow canary was quiet in its cage.

We visited him about once a month. We never planned to, but we'd happen to pass by the home on our way back from visiting friends or from the pool at the Abastos Sport

Center. He became more and more withered, and when autumn arrived Teresa said he looked like a leaf on the street, just any old leaf. He had moments of clarity. He could suddenly come out with something that made you realize he was present. Like when he mentioned the gorillas:

"You have to help the gorillas."

And we laughed at him, because who could help the gorillas?

Inés didn't visit him. When we brought it up with her, some mornings at the market or by the mailboxes in the entryway, she'd say she'd done her part.

One day in September, the gorillas escaped. The papers said the male had "planned it." It also quoted a zoologist, who said that for an animal to do something so extreme, for it to be capable of planning something like that, there must have been deep suffering. Teresa and I speculated over how it happened. He had taken the female and the children with him. Behaved in a threatening manner with the staff at feeding time, then fled with his family. They had taken the road through the Viveros Gardens, toward the sea. Across the bridge made of old railroad sleepers and onward, under the palm trees where the pigeons perched and the ground was flecked with droppings. Mild September wind, gorillas en route to the sea. Taking the sidewalk past the Jaime Roig bakery, the laundromats and video stores. The Creole chicken place. The city's edge, singed and unstructured. A building here, another there, fantastic cathedrals in the desert. The creaking tram to the right, diggers to the left. Ahead: the sea.

They shot him in the back. Once he'd fallen to the ground, it was easy to corral the wife and children. They were put back in their cages and died a few weeks later. Antonio died that same week, and we heard Inés muttering on the balcony: This was when he'd die, of course, now that she'd finally gotten rid of him – a quick drop and a sudden stop, as though he were full of the devil.

He doesn't mean to look sad; the expression creeps up on him.

"It's your own fault," she will say. "You're the one who hooked up with the cleaner. You crossed the line. It serves you right that she killed Marilyn."

He knows her expressions inside out. Her nostrils flare somewhere around "the line," her voice rises to a falsetto when she says "Marilyn." He raises his hand, to stop the rush of words. He doesn't want Jessica's blood pressure to skyrocket. Not now, not while they're on a nice, peaceful terrace, sharing some sort of vacation.

But if she keeps it up, he'll be sick. Not from sorrow and not from rage. But from nausea. He'll be sick on his clothes and in the hollow of her low-cut top. The sick will contain everything: the patriarchy and the establishment he's always had to answer for, and bad, half-digested pizza, pure shit that hasn't yet moved through the bowels.

But Jessica doesn't bring up Marilyn, or the line. Instead, she changes the subject, talking about the glass-bottomed sightseeing boat that travels around the island. Two departures a day, one after breakfast, one after lunch. The one after breakfast is better because the sun is still low in the sky.

He chews. Slowly, because the doctor said he needed to absorb the nutrients. Eat in moderation, slowly, and in good company, if possible. "Company," he'd replied. "Company has never been a problem for me. You get the company you deserve."

It was an unnecessary and conceited thing to say, he thinks, in retrospect. If you got the company you deserved, he wouldn't be here with his wife.

He swallows.

The waitress walks by. She has beautiful calves. Elongated. Hard-soled velvet shoes and a slow gait, making her way across the terrace and toward the sea and the horizon. A promising woman, perhaps. Nothing he'll let go of easily. He decides that, by dawn, he'll be between her thighs.

"Take the doctor's advice seriously, Clemente."

"I do."

"You either have your health or you don't."

"I probably have it."

"Consider your face and your physical condition. Your trauma."

"Are you saying I'm traumatized?"

"What if we took a trip around the island tomorrow? In that glass-bottomed boat."

Let's keep trauma out of this, he wants to say. He agreed to take a vacation with her, after all. He shut down his computer and stowed it in the security deposit box along with his BlackBerry. He spent two hours in Madrid traffic with her next to him before driving 500 kilometers to Dénia and installing himself in line for the hydroplane that took them to the island. He listened (listened!) to her, so attentively he almost convinced himself this would, in fact, be a nice vacation. And to keep the peace, he should say of course they should take a trip on a glass-bottomed boat.

Of course, Jessica! Of course we should take that trip. On the glass-bottomed boat. And if she feels like sucking him off in the bathroom, well that's just dandy. He can stash some paper plates in the camera bag to put under her knees, so she won't have to kneel in unidentifiable fluids.

"So, what do you say?"

"About what?"

"About the glass-bottomed boat."

"I don't know."

"Think about all there is to see."

"Fine."

"I'll make the call."

The sun is about to set. The terrace empties. Jessica fingers her mobile phone as she arranges the boat ride. He knows how many times he's looked down her top: three. The ocean view keeps catching his attention, too, but he's not keeping track of that. The waitress has a gap between her front teeth, but he hasn't decided whether or not it's unbecoming. Nausea rises and sinks inside him, and each time it nudges his throat, he helps himself to another mussel, chews and forces it down. Whenever he tries to contribute to the conversation, she responds with an accusatory look. He must have done something wrong today. Best he shut up, then. Like the Marilyn on the poster in the living room, just shut up and smile, don't risk your neck.

"Have you taken your pills?"

The waitress walks by.

"I said, have you taken your pills?"

"What?"

"Your pills?"

He finds them in his pocket, washes them down with wine.

Jessica signs the check. The waiter stands beside her, holding a silver tray with fluted edges.

"I'd like a cup of coffee," he tells him.

"You should've thought of that earlier," Jessica says. "The bill is settled."

She puts the pen on the tray and the waiter leaves. He takes a cigar from his inner pocket.

"It's no smoking," she says.

He lights up, puffs, and waits for the waitress to come over to his table, bare the gap between her teeth and tell him there's no smoking.

A romantic island, the ad said. No poop in the water, Jessica said. Sandy Rogers is playing. A few German or English tourists are on the dance floor, awkwardly pawing at each other. Their pants are wrinkled. He should say something nice to Jessica, be generous, make up for crossing the line. They're on vacation, after all. But she's speaking so quickly and intensely, about the patriarchy, about the patriarchy and the establishment and the whole crooked bunch conspiring to keep her from getting the position she wants at work. He can't remember what position it is and doesn't dare ask. She's probably told him several times, and when she's on a rant it's best to look out over the ocean and shut up. Think of the waitress's thighs, maybe about Blosom.

Unlike Jessica, Blosom had nothing against the patri-archy. At least that's what she said. She liked sex and money and had no problem with cleaning – no need for things to change on her account. The establishment was bad though, she said. She'd always had a hard time with the establishment, and when she said this, it made him feel uneasy. He didn't exactly know where he stood – if he, considering who he was, could be counted among the patriarchy or the establishment, or if he was a bit of both. He tried to think of shipping containers instead. Deadlines. Staff to be hired and fired, letters of credit and favorable interest rates. But his thoughts never stayed with the favorable interest rates, they glided along Blosom's throat, down into the dip between her collarbones where a silver gecko hung. Down between her breasts and around her waist, down to that black ass. That black ass. It had cost her sweat, sweat, and more sweat – at least that's what she'd say when he admired it. It was all she had, she'd say, and he'd respond that if he'd been a woman and was allowed to have one thing in life, he'd want an ass like that. She'd swat him with a duster when he said that. Friendly, but firm. His sex would ache, and he'd go after her. Into the bedroom with the blinds that were kept shut until Jessica came home at five.

· Of course he shouldn't have done it. Shouldn't have followed Blosom. Shouldn't have named the cat after the Marilyn on the poster. Shouldn't have betrayed Jessica, shouldn't be alive at all. He should have let himself be castrated and buried alive. That's what you expect of people nowadays – to just lie there and take it. That, and no bullshitting. But bullshit – as everybody knows – is impossible to get rid of. Even Jessica knows that: you can't avoid the bullshit and get straight to the fundamentals, you have to go through the bullshit. Go through the chaff to get to the grain of wheat, if you find it at all.

That black ass. He pictures it and it's an escape from the conversation, a door leading straight out into eternity. Blosom had said:

"It's basically all I have."

Right. He knew what she had. He could count it on one hand. A room in his and Jessica's house; a contract for domestic services bearing his signature; a suitcase with stickers from her Caribbean hometown, Livingston; five kilos of clothes; and forty-three euros in savings.

Mostly she ironed. No, in fact, she ironed all the time, because Jessica gave her mountains of ironing to try to keep them from ending up in bed. Mountains of ironing, and lists of things to be dusted. She liked saying it: *Blosom, don't forget the skirting boards behind the sofa!* Once, she bought a frog magnet and stuck it to the refrigerator along with a note that read: *Blosom, dust the skirting boards behind the sofa,* and even though Blosom dusted them, of course she did, Jessica refused to take the note down. It was fine where it was, she said.

The waitress's footsteps. Jessica has stopped talking and is looking at him. He's puffing. Blowing smoke in her direction. She digs around in her handbag. Takes out a pillbox and clasps it.

"You're so absent," she says.

"Me?"

"You."

He keeps puffing, looks out over the ocean. Soon it will be dark.

"Eh."

"Look. The pharmacist gave me these pills. I'm not really sure what they are, but they're some sort of happy pill. I take them occasionally."

"Really?"

"Yes. You can borrow them."

She smiles at him, and for a moment her arms relax and her chest slumps toward the table.

"Go ahead. Borrow them."

"Thank you, but pills aren't what I need."

Her face tenses up. Her mouth purses and her eyes go hard. Her breasts hoist up.

"What do you mean by that?"

"I mean: pills aren't what I need."

"OK. What is it that you need, then? Love?"

The waitress goes into the kitchen. The doors swing behind her.

"Maybe."

He shouldn't have said anything. Love wasn't even what he was suggesting. He needed her to go away.

"You know what, you're a dirty pig."

"Is that so?"

"Yes, you are. And I'll say it again: it serves you right that it ended the way it did. Blosom knew how to mess with people, oh yes. If there was one thing Blosom knew, it was how to mess with people."

He tries to look unfazed. He looks out over the ocean, his gaze gliding along the horizon, hoping the tears will stay in their ducts. But his face grows hot. From across the terrace he can hear the waitress's laughter. It peals. Shimmers. A pearly laugh spilling from a woman with thighs dusted with mother-of-pearl. Maybe she's called Perla. He once met a woman called Perla. Did he seduce her? He supposes so, he can't remember.

"I'm leaving," Jessica says. "You can sit here and dream about Marilyn, or the cleaner. Did you give her her severance pay, by the way?"

"I don't know, Jessica. I don't remember."

"If you didn't pay her, I don't think you should. I mean, killing Marilyn like that. How the poor thing must've suffered."

Her chest slumps again, insofar as fake breasts can slump, and for a moment she looks truly sad. She is, in spite of her venom, pretty when she's sad. The sadness refines her angular beauty. He feels like telling her she should be sad more often, genuinely sad. But she gets up, drains the glass of mineral water, and straightens her pink linen pants.

"I'm off."

She heads for the exit. He gets up.

"Jessica!"

"Yes?"

She turns toward him.

"How much longer do we have left?"

"Two weeks."

He sits back down.

Beyond the harbor, the mussel beds are mute.

That day (a day he would sooner or later eject from his memory, the way a stomach ejects vomit), she cleaned as usual. There was nothing to suggest anything would happen, aside from the marshy smell in the house, which he now identifies as a bad omen. There was something with the pipes that day. You could blame the soap plants, say they were rotting and giving off a smell, but actually it was the plumbing. Blosom joked about it.

"It's the Mr. and Mrs.'s plumbing that stinks. They're connected somehow, and the shit gets in, but it can't get out."

He replied: "That's marriage." An affliction, you don't get Venice without the stink.

She ran the feather duster over the cherrywood bureau. Grimacing from the stench.

"Whatever the case, Clemente. One of these days, I'm going to take this into my own hands and call a plumber. I live here too, after all."

She carelessly ironed Jessica's pile then went up and tried on Jessica's clothes. Yellow light filtered through the window. Jessica wouldn't be home for another two hours.

He leaned against the doorway. Said:

"Siesta?"

"Siesta?"

"Yes. Siesta?"

"I'm cleaning."

"You're cleaning?"

"Yes. I'm cleaning."

Marilyn rubbed up against his ankle.

"I want you."

Her back to him: irritating. Her fussy way of putting hangers on the rail. He tried again:

"I pay well."

"It's not that, Clemente. I'm cleaning."

"And anyway, I love you."

"I'm cleaning."

"Listen to me, Blosom. If it was only about sex, I could've taken the car, driven down to Casa de Campo, and nailed any one of those whores."

"Yes. That's exactly what you would've had to do. Take the car, drive down to Casa de Campo, and nail any one of those whores."

He took a banknote out of his pocket, threw it on the floor. She continued hanging up Jessica's clothes. He took out another note. And another and another, until she bent down and picked them up.

Post-coitus. The money on the floor was gone, as was she. Only a puddle on the pink rug remained, a souvenir to kiss the soles of Jessica's feet. He searched the house for her.

103

"Blosom?" He found her in the cellar with the plumber. He had a spanner hanging at his side; Blosom had bed hair and the money was stuffed in her panties. That's what she usually did: she'd walk around with the notes for a day or two, then use the money to buy cigarettes from the grumpy old woman at the cart outside El Corte Inglés.

She said:

"Juan here has come to fix the system."

"Let's call it the pipes," he replied.

"The system," said Blosom.

"The system," Juan the plumber said.

They looked at each other. The two of them at him. Him at the two of them. Eventually the plumber bent down and began to screw the pipe.

"If the system gets clogged," he said, changing tools, "and fills up with dirt and grease and you don't do anything about it, then you get a big fat clump that gets in the way and clogs everything up."

"Is that so?"

"Yes. You could say the system's a constipated fucker."

He searched his pocket for a cigar. Blosom looked at him. At Juan the plumber, and then back at him. He lit the cigar.

"And what does a cockroach like you charge for flushing out a constipated fucker?"

"Eighty euros."

"Well then. At least it's less than the price of a mediocre screw in this house."

He went up to the office, opened his calendar. Two thirty, a video conference with Aldous. Aldous would be there on the screen, tanned and wearing a white linen shirt. He would talk about rock and oil, women and bootleg liquor. There were ten minutes to go. He rested his head against the pipe that ran past his desk. Sometimes, you could hear the water gushing.

Today, you could hear Blosom and the plumber.

She said, down there, that if the system was plugged with grease, it was symptomatic of what was happening in this house. The plumber said to go on, he didn't mind her talking.

"Get it off your chest, it's easier to talk psychology with a plumber than plumbing with a psychologist."

They laughed. He thought he heard the plumber spit on the floor. Blosom snickered.

"They're the worst," the plumber said. "The slime that lives inside a BMW, in the houses in this area. The system, the establishment, well, the slime. If you want to do the world a favor, neutralize it."

"How?"

Through the pipes, Blosom sounded expectant.

"Well. Grab him, lay him out on a board, and castrate him, then stuff his junk in his mouth like the soldiers in Afghanistan did with the Russians. You know. Sew him shut. You could cut the lady's tits off."

Silence. He pressed his ear harder to the pipe. Blosom said something he didn't catch, but she sounded grave.

The plumber said if she was whoring herself to the system, that was her problem. If she wanted to fill herself up with gunk, why should he weigh in? And again, he said, what was the point of any of this bullshit? What difference would their talking make? Maybe those two were already sitting upstairs, Mr. and Mrs., the grease-clogged powers that be. Screw them. Screw them right in the ear.

It went silent. Then there was a gentle rushing in the pipes. Fifteen minutes later, he heard the plumber's car back out of the driveway and drive off.

*

Where did that waitress get to? The cigar has been smoked to the butt, and he's lighting a fresh one. If smoking is forbidden, the least you can expect is for someone to comment on it. The restaurant is empty. The staff start cleaning, stacking chairs and wiping down tables. The plasma screen at the bar is showing a program that pokes fun at politicians in Madrid. He listens, sipping the liqueur the waiter placed in front of him, perhaps as a consolation. On-screen, they're talking about Zapatero and the leader of the opposition. They are joking, and the channel seems to skew left, but they cross the line when they say the leader of the opposition's mouth looks like a butthole. He thinks it's distasteful, and considers asking them to change the channel. But soon, the program is interrupted by a Martini ad. In it, a waitress brings a tray to a man sitting in a restaurant. She sets the glass in front of him, turns around, and walks away from the man and the camera. But a thread from her skirt has gotten stuck in the table, and as she walks, her skirt unravels. Row by row, until you can see the edge of her panties, then Martini's logo superimposed on her ass.

Suddenly the voice appears, mild but rough as sandpaper:

"There's no smoking here."

He looks up.

With one hand on her hip, she repeats:

"No smoking."

"Really? And what are you going to do about it?"

"I guess I'll have to arrest you."

He laughs. She laughs too, or smiles, without opening her mouth, and he can't see the gap.

"Arrest me," he says. "Do it. Arrest me."

Imagine being allowed to believe you're something. Being allowed to believe that in spite of everything you aren't half bad. Being allowed to withdraw from your wife, from those enhanced lips and pointy breasts pointing at you, like the masses pointing at the guilty party. Being allowed to partake in the good life, rise up from your early grave, reach out and steal an ounce of sweetness from life's grapes, or perhaps, for a moment, do without life's fecal stink.

When her shift is over, they go back to her place. She lives in a small apartment above the tunnel where the buses go. She has a bed with a lemon-yellow (not bile-yellow, lemon-yellow) bedcover and a lot of pillows. She has a teddy bear, which he squeezes, and she laughs (finally he sees the gap – its width is unbecoming, but she has that pelvic bone that sticks out a bit and gives her body a rounder, more harmonious shape). He takes off her white apron and black dress. He pushes away the image of Blosom. He pushes away the image of Marilyn's wide-open eyes in the pressure cooker. He thinks about the Martini ad. But when he comes, he's thinking of the leader of the opposition. He can't help it – the image flickers past and he gets caught up in it, rolls around in it, and doesn't push it away until he pulls out of her.

He sleeps, wakes. It is dawn. The waitress is quiet in the sheets. He tries running his hand over her, wonders if she'll keep lying there, just breathing, like Marilyn used to do. She doesn't. She wakes up. Opens her eyes and looks at him through her eyelashes, which are clumped with mascara.

"Have you ever been in love?" she asks.

"What?"

"Have you ever been in love?"

"What does that matter?"

"Have you?"

He sighs.

"First, I fell in love with Marilyn, the Marilyn on the poster, and then with Marilyn the cat. Then I loved Blosom, but Blosom put Marilyn in the pressure cooker. Now all I have is Jessica."

The waitress laughs. She laughs with her head thrown back and the gap between her teeth is unbecoming. She can't have understood an ounce of what he said, but even so she's laughing so hard her breasts are bouncing. A David Lynch movie comes to mind, the one with two old, wicked people sitting in the back of a car, laughing at a naive girl's unhappy fate. He gets out of bed.

"I'm leaving."

"That's seventy euros. If you have anything to spare."

She has rolled onto her stomach and is hugging the pillow. He tosses the notes on her back.

"Keep the change," he says, and leaves.

He goes down to the harbor. The fishing boats are coming in, and boxes of moray eels are being dumped on the rocks. The boat with the glass bottom is the furthest off. Waves roll in, and the boat rises up and tugs at its mooring. Then it's yanked down. The fishermen unravel the nets and the sea snakes wriggle on the rocky slabs.

"Are these edible?" he asks one of the fishermen.

"Sure. Fried or boiled. My wife makes them. Five minutes in the pressure cooker, just long enough for them to die and get nice and hot."

He strokes his beard. Chuckles, as do the fishermen beside him.

"I had a cat once. It ended up in the pressure cooker, too."

"Is that right?"

"Yes. Just long enough for her to die and get nice and hot. Then I opened it up."

"Is that right. Well, you hear all sorts. People putting cats in washing machines and watching them through the glass. Seems strange is the new normal these days."

The fisherman's hands are brown. They're spotted. They're unraveling the nets.

The fisherman looks at him. Right in the eye, and his gaze is as cold and blue as ice.

"Me, I think it's cruel. I don't think you should've put your cat in the pressure cooker."

The fisherman blows his nose into his hand and flings the snot away.

"She was like a daughter to me."

"Who? The cat?"

"Yes."

He stops his unraveling.

"Uh. We've got things to do here."

He stays put. The fisherman builds a wall of silence between them. The sea snakes on the rocks are still moving – slow-slithering death spasms. The glass-bottomed boat continues to tug at its moorings, and each time the rope strains, the wood from the dock groans.

"She was like a daughter to me," he repeats. "Marilyn."

The fishermen exchange glances, wipe their fingers on their blue outfits, and pack themselves and their things into the boat. They leave the sea snakes on the rocky slabs. They start the engine and sail away without looking back. Now would be the time to undress. To wash the waitress's fluids off, go home, and lie down with Jessica. But not before floating around on his back for a while, taking in the veil of clouds above the island, the dawn.

But in all honesty, he doesn't believe in dawns. He believes in ugliness and masculinity and femininity, because he has looked deep into their eyes and what you've seen in their depths, you have to trust in for the rest of your days, whether or not you want to. He trusts in the bullshit, too. He trusts in the bullshit more than in the grain of wheat. He knows the bullshit, has only ever longed for the grain of wheat. Diffuse, unfixed longing. Like a cat who has spent his whole life in a green room, dreaming of blue. He laughs out loud.

She grabbed Mickey Mouse's head and pressed it to her chest. She looked up at me and smiled. Behind her were the chestnut trees of Retiro Park, the sun filtering through the leaves.

It was a beautiful afternoon.

Mickey Mouse reached for her, said something in a thick Peruvian accent.

"Come on," I said.

"Can Mickey come with us?"

"No."

I gave him a coin and said that was enough now. He should go find some children instead. That was why he was here, wasn't it?

We went to the Peruvian restaurant on Ventura de la Vega. There was something about a Peruvian accent, she said, it had something that you in Spain did not – especially you Madrileños.

"Your language is so heavy," she said. "Like a big bull turning around slowly. That's what you're like. Heavy, slow, and you lisp. You're testy, too. Imagine being jealous of Mickey Mouse – ha!"

"What's your point? Are you saying you want Peruvian Mickey for dessert?"

The waiter came over, and we ordered.

*

After the food, she forgot about Mickey and started talking about her sister and Juanito.

"Just think," she said. "Everything comes down to chance. I'm sure if Juanito had proposed to my sister when something fun or at least halfway stimulating was happening, she would've said yes."

I thought of Juanito. He had wet-look gel in his hair and in summer he wore a linen suit. I'm not gay, but I thought he looked all right. The linen shirt was high-necked, like a mafioso's or that guy who writes songs for Elton John.

"Yeah," she said. "Juanito should've proposed on a day when my sister was in a good mood. Instead he proposed after work, when she came home all tired and grumpy and had a headache. And do you think he'd fixed anything to eat, something tasty? Lit candles, or even done the dishes? No, he was just standing there in that mess with a smile on his face. Holding out a square box, assuming she was gonna say yes."

We laughed. I pictured Juanito getting rejected in that high-necked linen shirt of his, holding out his box toward her sister.

"But it wasn't really chance that made her say no." I said. "It was bad timing."

"I guess you could say that. Juanito messing up."

We ordered more wine. It was hot outside and people were walking around. There were a lot of tourists around. You could catch swells of different languages. Some just sat and stared. A moped drove by. I wondered when to propose to her.

"How would you like to be proposed to?" I asked.

"Me?" she smiled. "I don't know. But it should be fun. Something exciting, that sets my blood on fire."

"Sets your blood on fire?"

"Yes. I'm not getting married if there's no fire in my blood."

"You're intense," I said.

"That's what they say," she said and looked pleased.

She went to the bathroom and I thought now might be the time to propose, because she'd brought up the thing with Juanito and we were definitely feeling carefree. Maybe I could ask if her blood was on fire. And if she said it was, then I could take that as a yes. I kept turning it over in my head. I didn't have a ring. It wouldn't be a real proposal.

Then she came back and said she'd gotten her period. And had to go home because she didn't have anything with her.

I paid – the question had resolved itself.

That night and the whole next day I mulled it over. Did she say that stuff about Juanito because she thought it was time for me to propose?

"Of course she did," said Pedro. "Propose, for God's sake. Get your thumb out of your ass."

"And what about the fire? She said her blood had to be on fire. I don't know how to set her blood on fire."

"You don't know how to set your own girlfriend's blood on fire?"

"Um. Yeah, of course I do. But still. You know."

"What about a bullfight? You can propose right when the matador kills the bull."

I thought about it.

"You're right. That would be unforgettable."

"It totally would."

"And sort of symbolic. It'd be like saying: Take this ring and kiss life goodbye."

Pedro laughed at my analysis.

"You're too deep," he replied. "You lost me."

A bull dying. Me offering a box. It felt inappropriate somehow. But Pedro was right, I did overanalyze things. Pedro wasn't into analyzing things. Neither was she. I hadn't actually ever heard her analyze anything. I suppose that was what I liked about her.

I booked tickets for San Isidro. April fifteenth, at Las Ventas.

She was as happy as a kid. She wore the same red blouse she'd worn on that day in the park with Mickey Mouse. We bought cotton candy, which she ate, and it made her mouth sticky. Someone in the line said Almodóvar was there, too. There was a white limo parked on Calle Goya, toward the intersection. Maybe it was his.

"Almodóvar's limo is over there," I said.

"He doesn't use limos," she said. "He takes taxis like everybody else. Look, it's those Mickey guys again!"

There were three of them in a row, by one of the entrances.

I led her to a different entrance, and then we were inside. We made our way through the corridors. People were streaming in, and there was something euphoric about them, like the moments before death or an orgasm. The sand in the arena was smooth. The sound faded in and out, smells rose from the crowd. Sweat, tobacco, anticipation. The sun was on its way down. Someone was drinking red wine from a skin. I wondered how many people had a boner right at this very moment. I whispered to her:

"I wonder how many people have a boner right now."

We took a seat in the second row. She bumped into me with the cotton candy and my shoulder got sticky. I don't think I was the only one she bumped into, because the people around us were glaring. I could feel the box in my pocket. In my other pocket were the joints I'd rolled. I didn't know if we were going to smoke before, after, or throughout. The risk was she'd feel sick. She'd never been to a bullfight, and we were sitting pretty close. I decided to save them. Then we could smoke them in Retiro Park after she'd said yes.

The first bull entered. He was large and strong and black, weighing in at 480 kilos, and he came from Valladolid. She said he'd probably only eaten acorns and grass his entire life, had probably inseminated countless cows. In other words, he was a happy bull.

During the first *veronica*, the audience applauded. It had been so close to the horn. Voices around us whispered: This was going to be special, this one, with such a brave bullfighter and the bull, of course, the bull. During the next *veronica*, she whispered that the horn had actually nudged his vest. Her eyes were wide open, and I wondered if her blood was on fire.

A murmur rippled through the silence. The movements on the sand were heavy, dull, and soft. The box was in my pocket. Mine had rounded corners, because Juanito's had been sharp.

She put her hand on mine. I didn't feel carefree, and I didn't think she looked carefree anymore. Had the moment passed me by? She sat there, her sticky cotton-candy lips in a pout.

The joints, I thought. I lit one and we passed it back and forth. It settled softly around my head. And the matador took his place in the ring. His vest was dark green and embroidered with gold. The fabric was rising and falling with his breath, and I thought: Stay right there, let me sit here and breathe, wrapped in cotton wool, her hand on mine.

The silence again. That black body, the steps and the sand kicked up and the sword raised. Raised, plunged, and withdrawn.

That's when I should've proposed, but the opportunity slipped through my fingers, gone in a flash. A murmur rose around us. I lost focus, slid around inside my brain. I looked up at the audience, couldn't help but wonder where Almodóvar was sitting. The horses dragged the body away and the rakes came out. Bull number two was on his way in.

"I'm going to vomit," she said.

"You've probably had too much cotton candy," I said.

"I gotta get out of here."

We made our way through the aisles. I'd blown it. Cotton candy, marijuana, sun, and blood. Perfect for a proposal, or to hurl.

"Let's go to the park," she said. "At least there'll be shade."

We lay down under a tree in Retiro. It was a chestnut, and when I squinted, the leaves moved toward the light. It was beautiful, backlit like that. Everything was beautiful in the backlight. The world should be seen backlit. In the distance, some boys were kicking around a football. It wasn't too hot in the shade. It was just right. I fingered the box in my pocket.

And then he appeared. That big soft body and those polka-dot clown pants. That cheap plastic mask and that black nose, which wasn't even round but pointy, like it was homemade.

"Mickey Mouse!" she shouted. "Mickey Mouse! You have no idea what I've been through."

He sat next to us on the lawn, and she told him about the bullfight.

"Well, Spaniards are cruel," Mickey said.

"Peruvians are backward," I said. "Having to come here and work as Mickey Mouse and all."

She glared at me and patted Mickey.

"He's just a little jealous," she said. "It's nothing to worry about. I like Mickey Mouse *and* Peruvians."

"Where are you from?" Mickey asked.

"Catalonia."

"That's Spain, isn't it?"

"No. I didn't learn Spanish until I was fifteen. At home we were only allowed to speak Catalan."

"No shit," said Mickey.

"Yup," she said.

"So what's it like in Peru?" she asked.

I knew what he was going to say: Beautiful and fun, but it was impossible to live there. That's what they say. And that's exactly what he said. She was listening wide-eyed, as though she'd never before heard the biggest clichés to come out of South America. Mickey kept talking. How long could it possibly take to say so little?

I lit a fresh joint, lay back down, and looked up into the tree.

Why do I love her so much? I wondered. There were other women out there who were better, and would have been a better match. Who kept wet wipes in their bag so they didn't have to walk around with a sticky mouth, who when seeing Mickey in the park didn't light up and get turned on. For instance. There were probably lots of women out there who were better than she was. Who you could talk to. Who didn't suddenly drift into their own world, break eye contact, and stop listening to what you were saying. And practically speaking, there were probably plenty of women who wanted children and had jobs. Permanent jobs, with a salary and routine. Not like her, who worked at her father's bar. Washing coffee cups. It's what she wanted to do, she'd tell you if you asked her. It was a good job. Social, as much coffee as you wanted, and great tips if you just let people pat your butt. Just? It was possible to have a girlfriend who didn't say things like that out loud. It was possible to have a girlfriend who wasn't making out with a Peruvian Disney character in the park right in front of you.

But it was what it was, as it always had been. The first time I saw her in the bar, that laugh that kept cutting through the clinking coffee cups. Her red-and-white polka-dot dress and thick Catalan accent. She had sat across from me with her coffee, saying I shouldn't have to sit here all alone. Then we'd fallen asleep in the room she rented above the bar and it was hot and our bodies stuck together. I think that's where we got stuck together for real, her and me.

In a small room in Chueca, the gay neighborhood, one hot night in June, as the cockroaches darted along the skirting boards.

"Mickey Mouse! What are you doing?"

Mickey Mouse's hand was on her breast. I thought: I'm gonna kill him. Fuck it, I'm gonna kill that pathetic Peruvian.

"OK," he said, and the plastic head turned toward me. "That was stupid of me. But she took my hand. I didn't do anything."

She shook her head. Then laughed. The gap between her teeth.

"I think that's enough Mickey for you," I said.

"Just a little more," she said. "It was nothing, right? Why do we have to be so boring? So closed off? It's so nice here in the park. I feel so happy. Carefree. It's like my blood is on fire."

"I'm going to go buy the paper," I said.

I went to the newspaper place at Independencia. I flipped through *Quo* and *Semana*. I peeked between the branches. I wondered what the hell I was doing. Leaving her with the Peruvian. But what can you do? Normal doesn't work with her. Everything was an experiment. That's what she'd say:

"Everything is an experiment. You have to stay newborn."

I went back after a while. She was alone under the chestnut tree. Mickey was gone.

"What about Mickey Mouse?" I said. "Did he leave already?"

"I didn't like him after he took off his mask. He shouldn't have taken off his mask. That was stupid of him."

"And your blood? Is it still on fire?"

"Maybe. A little, anyway."

I kissed her. Let the tip of my tongue slide between her front teeth.

Maybe this was the moment to take out the box.

MISERY PORN

It started with the ad, and the television set.

Brand-new 28˝ Philips TV with universal remote. One problem. The TV turns itself off after a while. Can be restarted after ca 5 mins, then it stays on for a long time before it turns back off. 200 kr, as is.

It only cost two hundred kronor, and the current owner's area code was 046, so it wouldn't be a long drive. Cheap, close, the only snag was you'd have to be ready well before the show came on. But I had time now that I was unemployed, so why not?

By the way, I'm one of those boring guys who always checks the TV listings in the paper and knows exactly what to watch.

I picked up the TV at an apartment building in Klostergården the very next day. I pressed two one-hundred kronor notes into the hand of the owner, a man my age smoking the last of a cigarette. Then I drove home and plugged it in in the living room, into the only TV outlet in the house. Soon I heard the sound of that kids' show *Bolibompa*, and then came the picture. The picture was good. The sound, too. After exactly five minutes, the TV switched itself off. I waited five minutes and turned it on again. It was the news and weather. I watched that, along with *One with Nature*, which was right after. The TV didn't turn itself off all night. I fell asleep to an American movie. I woke up at twelve thirty and turned it off, went upstairs to bed, then slept until ten the next morning.

The house was in an older suburb of Vallkärra, outside Lund. I'd inherited it from my grandmother, which was good, because right after she died my life turned upside down. I split up with my live-in partner Elsa and got fired from my job. I tried to get my boss to understand that I was depressed because of the divorce, or separation, rather, but he didn't listen. He said insulting the customers was crossing the line. It was a service job, and attitude was everything. If you were curt and grumpy, no one would eat at his restaurant, and that lost him money. In short: Thanks and good luck.

At the unemployment office, I registered as a job seeker in the culinary industry. No one had called yet, but I wasn't too worried. I had the house and unemployment benefits. And now I'd even found myself a cheap TV, so I didn't need anything – except Elsa in bed at night, in the morning over breakfast, and in the evening in front of the TV. Elsa would probably have laughed out loud if I'd shown her the TV that turned itself off after five minutes. We could've laughed together. Tossing her hair back, as she did, mouth open.

Elsa.

The next evening it was the same deal with the TV. A movie was starting at nine on Channel One. I switched it on five minutes before and lay on the sofa with a plate of sandwiches, a beer, and a pack of cigarettes. After five minutes it switched off. I waited, then I switched it on again. The movie began and I ate my sandwiches. The beer was cold and good. After the movie came a documentary about Iraq, and I fell asleep.

I woke up at two. I sat up on the sofa, pushed away the ashtray and the beer glass, and rubbed my eyes. They felt gritty. Then I carried the plate, the glass, and the ashtray to the kitchen. Standing at the counter, I noticed the sound coming from the TV. It was a woman crying. Sniffling and blowing her nose, then crying more. I put the butter and ham in the fridge, and the sound continued. What a weird movie, I thought. Such a long crying scene. I went back to the living room. And there it was – a woman sitting tall on a chair and crying on camera. A white Windsor chair in a large room with a dark wooden floor and deep-red curtains. A white rug on the floor and a dog at the woman's feet. You couldn't see the woman's face; her hair was in the way. I stood there for a second, waiting for the scene to end. But it kept going. The woman cried and the dog kept glancing up at her, doleful, not lifting its head. I switched to Channel Two. Sports. I switched back to Channel One. Now it was a rerun of *Sing-along at Skansen*. What was going on? I flipped through the channels to find the crying woman. Not because I cared, but still. Gone. Then I turned off the television and went upstairs to bed. Maybe I'd confused what I'd seen with images from a dream I was waking from. A hypnagogic image is what that's called. Or hypnopompic. I don't remember, I learned it in high school psychology.

I slept until eleven the next day. Then Elsa called, saying she was going to stop by to drop off some of my things. Nothing important. Underwear and a Lichtenstein picture. Some diving equipment and a sweater my sister had left at our apartment. Elsa hung around for a while. She said the house was nice. Well, she does like exposed beams and mirrored doors and large windows. Then she said what a shame it was that a bum like me was living here. I had neither the furniture nor the finesse to furnish it. Maybe for a second she considered getting back with me, coming to live in this lovely house and doing it up. Maybe she didn't, maybe she'd met someone new already. She put the IKEA bag full of junk on the floor and left. I watched her go. I've always liked her type. A nice walk, hair cascading down her back, softly slapping against it.

I had spaghetti with tomatoes and garlic for lunch. I swung by the mailbox and picked up the mail. Bills and ads. I thought about driving into town and doing the shopping. Then I fixed myself a cup of coffee and sat by the window, staring out at the garden. I could see a few neighbors poking around in their beautiful gardens. I should tend to mine, too. Grandma's roses, the raspberry bushes, and the holly.

In the evening, I turned on the TV. This time I didn't know what to watch, so I started channel surfing. I fell asleep. And again, I woke to the sound of someone crying. The TV was on, and the woman from the night before was back. On the same chair, in the same room with the cherry-print curtains. The dog at her feet. Crying and crying. It just kept going, and I let it run for a full half hour before I switched over to Two and then back again. Gone. My God, I'm losing it, I thought. Depression can make you lose it. See things. I thought: Tomorrow I'll google "symptoms" and "depression." See what comes up. I went to bed and had a strange feeling in my gut. I slept quite well anyhow, but when I woke up the next morning I had diarrhea.

The next day I went to the agricultural co-op and bought some gardening tools. A rake, a hose, a few things to dig around with in the beds, and a pair of orange and green gloves – too feminine for my taste, with those flowers at the wrist, but they were the only ones left, and they were cheap. I fixed myself an omelet for lunch, mixing eggplant and zucchini into the batter, like Elsa used to. I had a green salad and a beer with it. I ate out on the stairs to the terrace. The sun was warm. I was sitting pretty. Then I drank a cup of coffee from the morning brew and got going with the garden.

I'd been pottering for a while when a dog came running into my garden. It sniffed around, so I got up and took it by the collar to lead it out to the road. Maybe its master or mistress would be standing there looking lost. Leading the dog through the garden, I realized I'd seen it before. On the TV. It was the dog that sat at the crying woman's feet. I stopped, checked the dog's collar. Then I heard a voice calling:

"Rosebud!"

The dog ran off. I watched it go into the neighboring yard. A woman was raking her flower beds. The dog ran over and lay down beside her in a pile of earth. Was this the woman who'd been crying on my television? I wanted to go up to her and ask, but how would that have sounded?

"I've seen you crying on my television."

You can get locked up for less, and anyway, I didn't want to kick off my time here as the neighborhood nut. I waved and minded my own business. The next time I looked up, the woman and the dog were gone.

That night I set up a digital camera by the television. And I had a glass of red wine, maybe two, to help me sleep. But I didn't fall asleep. I was wide awake, waiting for the woman to appear and start crying. She didn't. An Ettore Scola movie droned on, then the presenter wished us a good night. Next came the time, and then nothing.

I turned it off and went up to bed, thinking I'd call the doctor the next day.

The next night, she was back. I nodded off, and when I woke up she was on-screen, sitting there, crying. I took a picture with the digital camera. Now it was documented. I went to bed, and a phone call from the Unemployment Office woke me up early. A job as a pantry chef had opened up a few kilometers outside of Åkarp. I took down the reference number and promised to email my application over that day.

I'd grown curious. I thought I might find an excuse to visit the woman next door, see if the interior was the same as the one on TV. I drove into Lund to go shopping. I went to the market and bought a fruit basket. Baby bananas from Thailand, mangoes, and a green, toad-like fruit I'd never seen before, but which the woman behind the counter said would be really tasty. Then I went to the liquor store and bought a bottle of sparkling wine from Veneto. It was a nice basket, the kind that puts a smile on a girl's face. I'd learned a thing or two in my time with Elsa, and even if I was no hotshot when it came to the dishes or cleaning, I could at least make a woman smile, and that was what mattered the most in the short run, or when all you wanted was an excuse to snoop.

I knocked on her door, and everything was as I thought it would be. There were deep-red curtains in the living room and a white rug, a white Windsor chair. There was a table, too, but that hadn't been on the TV. She put the basket on the table. She seemed happy that I'd stopped by. She probably thought I was courting her. We sat there, making small talk, exchanging glances.

"So, what do you do?" I said.

"What do you mean?"

"What do you do for a living?"

"Misery porn."

"Excuse me?"

"Misery porn. You know. People suffering."

"That's terrible. So, what, you torture people?"

"No, I just cry. Try to get people to buy it. I have a webcam, and I broadcast it on a local frequency."

"Is there anything in particular that's making you sad?"

"Yes."

"Aha."

I got up. So she was crying in the hope that people would watch, and if they enjoyed it they'd cough up some dough. There really wasn't anything more to say. Except that I must have picked her up on some strange frequency with my unusual television.

I went home. I slept well that night. I got rid of that TV the next day, took out some of the inheritance, and bought a plasma screen for ten large. I hung it next to the open fireplace, and from the sofa I had a view of the fire, the television, and the clock in the hall. Perfect.

A few weeks later, my childhood friend Joshu came to visit. He stayed in the guest room and was pretty independent. We settled into a sort of routine. He'd do his own thing during the day, then we'd reconvene on the terrace to smoke a cigarette before making dinner.

One evening I looked at him out there. Good and proper, I mean. I thought he looked pasty. Dark circles under his eyes. His hairline seemed higher. Joshu had looked pretty good as a teenager. Definitely better than me. And now here he was, the less happy one. Weather-beaten and wounded. Well, say what you like, but I haven't met many people who've lived it up like Joshu has. Girls left, right, and center. His poetry was forever being rejected. Next to him, I probably seemed like a real bore. With my chef's education and traditional Swedish food. And Elsa, who was one of those good girls. I was the only man she'd been with. I guess she was the only one I'd been with, too.

"What's that?"

Joshu pointed at the TV I'd dumped on Grandma's compost.

"Uh . . . Just some worthless old TV."

"You know TVs aren't biodegradable, right?"

We had a laugh. Then I said:

"Hey, by the way. You won't believe what happened to me."

"No way. *Something happened* to you? Spill."

"Stop it. You know I'm depressed, right?"

"Yes. Even more reason to go out. Have some fun. Screw around."

I didn't respond.

"OK. So, what happened?"

"Nothing."

"Tell me."

"Um . . . Just a girl who lives next door. She does misery porn."

"You're joking."

"No."

"So, what does she do? Torture people on camera?"

"You could say that. Only it's herself she's torturing."

I told him about my neighbor. The TV and the fruit basket. Her dog, which was called Rosebud, of all things. The crying.

"Well, well, well," said Joshu. "Comfort-seeking woman with lost childhood."

"How do you know that?"

"Why else would she have named her dog Rosebud? You should tap that. It'll be easy, like picking a ripe apple. You're a shoo-in. Come on, have a little fun. You and your depression."

After a few days, Joshu left. I was back on my sofa, staring at the fireplace, clock, and television. Sometimes I thought about getting out there and having a little fun. Having sex. Maybe he was right, Joshu, that sex is about energy, and the more sex you have, the more energy you generate. Now, I was on power saving mode, and if I didn't do something drastic I'd soon be drained. And the neighbor was right there. She'd checked me out when I'd visited her. And maybe I'd been insensitive when I'd thanked her and gone home, right after she'd said there was actually something making her sad, that it was the reason she cried. Maybe at the very least I owed her an apology.

I decided to go into Lund that afternoon. Maybe I wouldn't buy another fruit basket, but something else. A record, but that could go wrong. Flowers, but how fun were they. Then I thought of Grandma's garden. It was full of late-summer fruit. Blackberries. I could pick a basket of blackberries. They were beautiful – large and black and sort of moist. There was something melancholic about them, even with their sweetness. Maybe she'd make the connection. But what did I know about her sweetness? I could only hope it was there, inside the darkness. Like treasure waiting to be discovered or something.

I found a bottle of champagne in Grandma's basement. Moët & Chandon, just right.

My neighbor seemed happy that I'd turned up. We introduced ourselves this time. Her name was Aniara.

"What a beautiful name," I said.

"It's a hippie name," she said.

We started out by sitting there again, like last time, sort of sizing each other up. We sipped Grandma's champagne and ate the blackberries. They stained her mouth. Sexy, I tried to tell myself, even though I didn't really want her. I felt there was a cable inside me, a wire or a nerve, that wasn't hooked up right. Whenever I thought about sex, I thought of Elsa. It was absurd. I'd have to try and change that. Rewire myself, so to speak. If I could manage to have sex with another woman just once, then maybe the problem would be solved. Maybe I'd become like other men, who seemed to go around with a ball of fire in their chests, who could get hot for a girl in five minutes. Like Joshu, then.

" . . . and then I started to cry. Since then I haven't been able to stop."

"Excuse me?"

She gave me a funny look. I realized I'd been sitting there thinking about other things – sex, actually – while she'd presumably been sharing the root of her sorrow with me. I felt ashamed. I was the worst. I should really have just gone home. Seduction starts with listening, someone once said. It probably wasn't Joshu, but it was well put. I'd missed out without even thinking.

We sat in silence. A charged silence. The dog was asleep at her feet, and in front of us were the glasses with bubbles rising to the surface. Out in the garden, the sun was going down. You could see the plains and the willows, and the spires of the cathedral beyond them.

I plucked up the courage, reached out, and put my hand on her neck. Her earlobe. It was soft and downy. It was nice to touch. She stiffened, but only for a moment. Then she started to cry. Desperate and jerking, with her face buried in her hands.

"Oh, sweetie . . . "

I moved closer to her. I put my arm around her. She was thin, almost bony. I stroked her hair, whispered something in her ear. Suddenly her mouth met mine, and she pushed her tongue inside me. I got the hang of it quickly, even though her kissing was so unlike Elsa's. Elsa had smaller, plumper lips and sort of nibbled – her tongue didn't usually come into play for a while – but this, this was different. Passionate, you could say. And the tears that ran into our mouths were salty and gave the kiss a peculiar quality.

I undid her clothes and soon she was lying naked in front of me. She was pure white. She was beautiful – well, not exactly, but you know, to me she was a foreign landscape. How to begin, what to touch? Elsa had a dip between her shoulder and neck, a perfect dip to rest your head on and just sort of nuzzle, taking in her scent and letting your hands wander. Elsa smelled like freshly baked bread. We used to laugh about it sometimes, but that was her scent, like whole wheat rolls fresh out of the oven. Aniara had another smell. Milk, maybe. Or maybe it was just the association with white. And the unstoppable tears. The tears, all that salt on her face. Eyes swelling and saliva spilling from her mouth.

So she was lying there, naked, and I hadn't even taken my shirt off yet.

"Don't take it off," she said. "Let's do it like this."

I pulled down my pants and pushed into her. I was hurrying, because I didn't know how long my lust would last; I was afraid the tears would turn me off and I'd wilt like a flower and she'd start crying even more. There were some things you couldn't do to a woman, the first time. Or so I thought.

But I soon noticed that it wasn't turning me off at all. It had the opposite effect. The whole situation was actually a real turn-on, because she was naked and crying and I was clothed and yes, I actually felt strong. She was at my mercy. It was a new feeling. I slowed down. Whispered things in her ear, cautiously at first. Then I became bold and whispered more daring things, and in the end, I whispered terrible things that I'd probably never even whispered to Elsa. I'm pretty sure we came simultaneously. I mean "pretty sure," because you never really know if a girl has come, especially if it's your first time with her. But if she hadn't actually come, then she was a good faker. I think it was the strongest orgasm I'd ever had in my life, and somewhere inside me that orgasm lived on as joy, like a bottle of fizzing champagne. The Elsa cable had now been rewired. I'd found a new source of energy.

Well. Things never actually stay fizzy or joyful, that's for sure. But the feeling can last for a few moments, and it can replenish your energy reserves. That's nothing to be sniffed at.

The next night, I called Joshu.

"You have no idea," I said. And I told him. From start to finish, leaving nothing out.

"Damn," he said. "What'd I tell you? It's all gonna be different now. How about we go to Berlin for the weekend? Take ourselves out for a spin. I'll handle the hotel and the girls. You just come along for the ride."

"No," I said. "I've got Aniara now. Let me talk to her first."

"Your loss, man."

I told him about her sadness, and what had happened between us. This was important. I couldn't just bow out. This was really something.

"OK, you're right," he said. "She seems perfect. The sensitive type. It'll get on your nerves day-to-day, but you're heading for one hell of a sex life. Pedal to the metal. It'll be good."

We hung up. I called Aniara and invited her to dinner. Then I drove to the sushi restaurant by Botulf's and picked up food. To Lejonet & Björnen to buy mango sorbet and a bottle of sweet, sparkling Italian I'd pour over it. This marked the end of traditional cooking and Elsa habits. Now, space was wide open and I had my new spaceship, Aniara.

It was a typical love affair. Intoxicating and intense. At least that's what Aniara said – apparently she had more experience with these things than I did. Sometimes, I visited her web page at night and saw her sitting there, crying. Sometimes, it turned me on so much that I walked right over and knocked on her door. Later, she told me she hadn't turned off her webcam, and the number of visitors to her page had tripled since I came into the picture. I guess that felt good. Contributing to her success, I mean. But it was also dizzying to have sex knowing that out there in cyberspace five million people might be watching us.

I kept the pantry chef job in Åkarp, and thanks to Aniara and all the new energy charging through my life, it was smooth sailing. I began assisting the chef, suggesting new dishes. One of my suggestions made it through: that we have some special dishes in our restaurant that you couldn't find anywhere else. Like, on Thursdays we could serve a pasta dish with hand-cut tagliatelle.

"Do you have any idea how much that will cost in labor?" my boss said. "Having someone standing there cutting pasta with a knife? For sixty people?"

"I'll handle it," I said.

And I told Aniara about my project. She said it was brilliant and offered her help. We were there long into the night, twisting tagliatelle into small nests. Then we had sex on top of the sacks of grain in the pantry. Rough and clumsy, and it made me think of the spaceship.

I think it started to go downhill in October. There were bad omens in the air, Aniara said.

"Omens?" I said.

"Yes. That I'm going down."

I didn't understand what she meant. We had it so good. Did she need more stimulation? Maybe I didn't measure up. I suggested we travel, took out some of the inheritance and invited her to Stockholm for a long weekend. We rented a hotel room on Hötorget, in the blue building with the tall windows. The windows had gigantic frames, and Aniara sat in one of them while I popped the champagne.

"If we're not God, then we must at least be angels."

She said this naturally, as if slipping between worlds was something people just did. I guess I felt flattered by her way of speaking, or rather her carelessness, because it was proof she was allowing me into every aspect of her life. There weren't any solid lines between Aniara's outside and her inside. I was allowed in both worlds, and that was staggering.

But it was also hard, because the boundaries kept stretching. Crying-sex in front of the webcam wasn't enough anymore, she said we had to go further. I tried to explain to her that it wasn't necessary, as far as I was concerned – so far, our relationship had been like one long sexual march in thousand-mile boots. I'd had so much, I wouldn't need a refill for decades. I was happy with how things were. This made her laugh.

"You're so sweet," she said. "You use such nice words. Togetherness, thousand-mile boots, sexual march. Say something filthy instead."

"Whore."

She sighed. Slid off the windowsill and stood in front of me.

"The problem with you is that when you say something like that, you don't mean it."

"How can I mean it? I love you."

"And like every Tom, Dick, or Harry, you think love is the same thing as being nice."

"Aniara, you're scaring me. People like you are dangerous, for God's sake. To yourself and to others. You must be sick. You must feel terrible."

She laughed – and with genuine amusement, with one of those laughs that makes you feel ridiculous.

"You're a nice guy," she said. "But you're boring. You should do something with yourself."

I sat there, champagne glass in hand. The bubbles were rising to the surface. Those fine bubbles rising to that fine surface. My hand around the glass, my hand that wanted to be touching Aniara, making her happy. And she stood in front of me, with those dark rings under her swollen eyes, saying she didn't want all the fine things I wanted to give her. She wanted something else, something filthy. And what did I know about filth? Had I ever had been filthy? Wasn't I just a normal guy who wanted what people wanted most? A good life. A good relationship and a decent job. I'd never looked for all that darkness she was talking about. It was the kind of thing people worked to rid themselves of, not invoke. Yes, people paid astronomical sums an hour to get rid of that kind of thing. I thought: Aniara isn't my type at all. She belongs with sick people. I have to get out of here, I thought. Take my things and go back home to Vallkärra before it all goes to shit.

Aniara gulped down her glass and helped herself to more. We hadn't even toasted, and she was drinking the 800-krona champagne I'd bought with my inheritance as if it were mineral water. Her hair was tangled. She was thinner. I should get her to a doctor. Maybe give her a full-day spa package, so she could get her hair done, have a facial and a massage. Girls like that kind of thing. Aniara would like that kind of thing, too. Then we could have a nice dinner somewhere. Be a bit normal. A bit of normalcy, for God's sake, was that too much to ask?

"Name an animal you identify with," she said, standing by the window.

I was somewhat relieved by how normal the question was. It was one of those things normal people asked each other to make conversation. I answered quickly:

"A bird of prey."

"Which one?"

"A falcon. Or maybe an eagle."

She nodded thoughtfully.

"And why?" she asked.

I thought about it. Pictured those beautiful birds up in the sky.

"Because they can ride the thermal currents. And when they spot something they want, they dive down and take it. Slick. I like that."

I reached for her, but she pretended not to notice. Instead, she turned toward the window and looked up at the sky. Drank, looked up at the sky, emptied her glass. I was about to ask her which animal she identified with when she hopped down from the window and came over to me on the bed.

"I was thinking we could try something new," she said.

"But I thought . . . " I began.

"You should hit me," she said.

"What?"

"Hit me."

"You're joking."

"Try."

"I don't want to hit you!"

I felt my palms getting sweaty. Aniara tilted her head, gave me an arch look, and twisted a lock of hair around her index finger.

"'An eagle,' you said."

"And?" I said.

She laughed.

"An eagle soaring in the sky. Taking aim. Diving. Taking what he wants. I agree. It's a nice image. A strong image."

"Aniara, I don't know what you mean."

"Well, look at you. Listen to what you're saying."

"I still don't understand."

"You are not an eagle," she said, with a sudden chill in her voice. "You're a beetle trying to do acrobatics."

She turned and went back to the window. It seemed to go quiet, as though all the sound had disappeared – the buzz from the square, the traffic in the distance – as though everything had suddenly been soaked up by invisible cotton wool. I felt the heat rise to my cheeks, my forehead, and up toward my hairline. I looked at the window and the light felt too bright. A beetle trying to do acrobatics.

That's how the woman I'd desired most in my entire life had described me.

"Lay off, will you?" I said.

I thought my voice sounded metallic. My tongue tasted of iron.

"'Square beetle seeks thermal current on which to soar,'" she said, laughing. "That could be a personal ad for someone like you."

"You're cynical."

"You're square."

"I just want to have a nice time."

"And I just don't want to feel like I've been buried alive."

"Is the camera set up or what?" I said, walking toward her. "Do you want to set a new record? So you can get more banner ads on your page, earn more money? That's called prostitution, Aniara! Whoring!"

"That's better. You're improving."

She nodded sagely and filled her glass.

"You're sick!" I exclaimed.

I stared at her, pulling at my hair.

"I'm sorry, Aniara," I said. "I can't do this."

I was still shaking with rage as I went to pack my things. My bag was almost untouched, I'd only unpacked my toothbrush and toothpaste, which were in the bathroom. Brushing your teeth on arrival, something you do to feel fresh. One thing among many that a man would do to please Aniara. Something beetles do so that beautiful women aren't disgusted when they kiss them.

I don't know what it was. The alcohol, maybe. The unfamiliar environment, the hotel room that felt as though it were made for fleeting and tawdry encounters. Aniara's provocations, the image of an eagle on my retina overlaid with a beetle on its back, its legs scrabbling in the air. Something in me broke. The fluorescent light from the bathroom stung my eyes. There was a flickering, and I threw the toothbrush on the floor. I went over to the window where she was sitting and took her by the hair and dragged her across the carpet. She screamed, and I put my hand over her mouth. Soon she went quiet, and there was something new in her eyes when she looked at me. Appreciation. A spark that hadn't been there before. At first I thought I'd cry seeing her look at me like that, but then it surfaced, an aggression I couldn't explain after the fact, other than to say it must have been primitive, some remnant from another phase of humanity that shouldn't have stayed with us. That should've been tempered. So, I hit her. I hit her in the face. I saw my bloody hand and yet I didn't stop. I thought I'd ruined her nose because there was a crack, as if something had broken. But I kept going, and although it was terrible, it was also a relief. I can't explain the feeling any other way than that it was like a lake, or a dam, suddenly open. Like a body of water set free.

But soon the aggression ebbed and was replaced by disgust. I stopped. I bit my hand hard, focused on my own pain, sank down over her, and cried. I had the taste of mucus and blood in my mouth and I didn't know if it was mine or hers. She lay still beneath me. Shit, I thought. Shit shit shit. I've killed her.

There was a knock on the door. I got up, went to the bathroom, and looked at myself in the mirror. Wiped myself off with a towel, and opened up.

"Is everything OK?"

It was a woman in a blue uniform.

"Yes. Everything's OK."

"We heard a woman screaming. The people in the next room called down to reception."

I didn't know what to say. The woman stared at me.

"Is there a woman in this room?" she said.

I felt like laughing. It's all over now, I thought. They'll find her, and then they'll take me away. I pictured explaining how much I loved Aniara to a bunch of people in blue uniforms. Meanwhile she'd be there beside me, beaten to death. They'd laugh at me, and Aniara would laugh at me, too, even though she was dead. "Stupid little beetle," she'd whisper with her beaten mouth. "You hit me a little too hard, didn't you?"

"Would you be so kind as to let me in, so I can see if there's a woman in the room?"

The blue woman was trying to push past me when I heard Aniara's voice:

"Don't come in. I'm fine. Just fine."

The woman in blue stopped mid-step and gave me a quizzical look. Then she retreated to the door and said:

"If we hear any more from you . . . "

"Don't worry," I said. "It'll be perfectly quiet."

I couldn't imagine leaving the room that night. We'd planned on walking around Stockholm, eating at one of the restaurants Aniara knew. Maybe taking a boat somewhere, to an island, and spending the night. Whatever took our fancy, as usual. But I couldn't, I felt ashamed and disgusted with myself. In any case, Aniara's face was black and blue. Marred. When I looked at her, something in me lurched.

"I've hurt you," I said. "It's absurd. Look at you."

She smiled at me and blinked with the one eye. The room spun. I felt sick. Yes, I felt like vomiting on myself and on her.

Slowly, it dawned on me. There, in the hotel room with the large windows in Stockholm: Aniara was probably a masochist. I thought about Google again, that I'd have to search for that word, see what I found, read up on it so I could understand how she ticked. I thought about Joshu. If I'd told him about this, he would've said it was pure gold. A masochistic nymphomaniac. Pedal to the metal. But that's not how I felt. Because there was something egotistical about this whole Aniara thing. The recklessness in her surrender, the presumption that I set the limits and not actually hurt her. She could just *be*, taking pleasure in my roughness, but I was the one left to control the situation. And if anything happened, of course I'd be held responsible. Be labeled a sadist. I was no sadist. I didn't want to be a sadist. I wanted to be what I was, and I wished she would love me for it.

We spent two more days at the hotel. We ordered all our meals on room service, and the staff gave me funny looks when it arrived.

"Aniara. Say something, so they know I haven't beaten you to death."

"Something," she said from the bed.

We went back to Lund. Took a plane to Sturup and then the airport bus. It was foggy, and people had begun to look sallow, staring into nothing on the bus. Someone looked at Aniara's mangled face and then angrily at me. She seemed to be smiling to herself, as though she enjoyed people thinking of her as a beautiful victim, and me a hot-blooded hooligan.

Everything seemed to go back to normal, for a little while. The autumn rain came. It whipped the windows in Grandma's dining room and the willows out on the plains, their bare branches sticking straight up. Then the truck came and trimmed them and they looked like bones. I bought lumber from a farmer outside of Nöbbelöv and built a small shed in the garden. On Aniara's web page, the crying had intensified. When we met up, her eyes were almost always red-rimmed, but the bruises and swelling from the beating had begun to fade. The whites of her eyes were bloodshot, as usual. I tried to cheer her up, stay the course, but it wasn't easy.

"There's something you have to understand," she said. "This is the way I am. I'm happy when I'm unhappy. And if you make me happy, then I'll be unhappy."

I didn't really understand what she meant, but I stopped making an effort. Her psyche was like a labyrinth. If I made an effort, I'd only go more astray. End up lost, unable to find my way out.

I lit fires in the fireplace. Baked apple cake and made hand-cut tagliatelle. Kept up on the wines at the liquor store, and pumped iron for five minutes each morning.

Elsa came by one day. She brought her new boyfriend with her, a man in a suit who must've been at least twice her age.

"Hi," she said. "We just thought we'd pop by, Lennart and I."

"Did you now?"

"Yes. I told him you had those Finnish windows. He exports them to the continent."

"I see."

"Is it OK if we have a look around?"

"Of course."

I cracked open a beer and waited out on the steps. I watched Elsa through the window, going around with her potbellied Lennart. I thought Elsa looked ordinary.

Hair in a ponytail, wearing jeans, nothing to set her apart from any other girl. When I thought about it, I couldn't even remember the whole wheat smell in the dip by her shoulder.

"Thanks for letting us have a look," she said as they left.

"Thanks for letting us have a look," Lennart said and followed her out.

"It's nothing."

That same night, clouds rolled in from the west. The wind picked up, and I checked the weather on SMHI, which said there was almost certainly going to be a storm. I did a round of the garden, made sure the terrace roof was properly secured. Grandma had said it would come off sometimes and fly around in the neighbors' gardens. I thought it seemed loose and was just about to hammer in an extra nail when I heard Aniara screaming:

"You cheater! You fucking cheater!"

I looked down from the roof, and there she was. Wrapped in a sheet, barefoot, her hair on end in the wind. Her eyes were swollen as usual, and tears were streaming down her face, though maybe some of it was rain. She was all wet. The wind felt ice-cold. I jumped off the roof and went to her. She shrank.

"You're not coming anywhere near me. I hate you."

"But Aniara . . . I don't understand. Come on, let's talk it through."

"It's over, you fucker, do you hear me? I won't take any shit. I saw her."

"Who?"

"Her. Your ex-girlfriend. And her dad. You're one big fucking family now. Home sweet home. I won't stand for that shit!"

I reached out and tried to get hold of her. I pulled her toward me, and she scratched my face. Pulled my hair. Screamed and scratched like a wildcat. I picked her up and carried her into the house. Wrestled her down onto the floor, pushed myself inside her. It was sick, the same sick feeling I'd had in Stockholm. Maybe I'd been hoping it would ebb away. Behind us the open door was thwacking in the wind.

The terrace roof must've been torn off, because when I came out a few hours later, it was gone. I went looking for it in the neighbors' gardens, thinking maybe it had blown into one of them. But it was gone. I never found it again.

I felt a growing reluctance about the whole situation. There was nothing soft or unforced in our relationship. Nothing was simple and clear like you want everything to be. You want love to be love. Lust, lust. Rage, rage. Relationships, relationships. The end, the end. No borderlands. No limbo. No vague contours, no emotional twilight. I wasn't used to functioning like this, I felt like I was losing clarity and energy. I mean, I was a regular guy. Square. A guy who'd always turned off the light before sex, who thought happiness was the goal of life, and who was happy as long as there was good food and good company. Yes, if I were to write a personal ad, that's probably exactly what I'd write.

The encounters between Aniara and me were a sort of concession on her part, and a frightening realization on mine. The thing with Elsa and Lennart, to give a minor example. How could she actually believe that was Elsa's dad? And in any case, what would we have been doing? Discussing the details of a wedding? It was absurd. It was like Aniara was performing, making up situations to add tension and spice. It dawned on me that I couldn't keep up with her. However good the sex had been, we'd get to a point where we couldn't go any further. I would gravitate toward a normal life. With children, maybe. A normal relationship. She would keep rising into the atmosphere, seeking new heights.

I could tell it was coming to an end. All that energy had sort of consumed itself.

Aniara became more and more destructive. Once, she knocked on my door and reached out her bleeding wrists. As I was disinfecting them, I saw the wounds weren't deep at all, just deep enough for the blood to flow. Anyway, everyone knows it's not easy to kill yourself by slitting your own wrists. You practically have to be a surgeon to pull that off.

"Aniara," I said. "Why are you doing this?"

"My clients, you know. They want something more fun than a girl sitting on a chair, crying."

"But cutting yourself. There has to be a limit?"

"Does there?"

I began to prepare a way to end it. Sometimes I tried to convince myself she was getting tired of me, too. I was too vanilla for her. There had to be men who were more interested in taking her bait than I was.

But the more I tried to cool our relationship down, the more she seemed to wrap herself around me. She packed a bag and came over to my place. She set up the webcam above our bed. Then she lay there, crying. She was overly happy while we were having sex and when I came, and when I left, she was sad again, like an unhappy marionette.

"We should do the Stockholm thing again."

"You've only just healed."

"We have 5,000 visitors a day now. We just need to keep doing what we're doing. Then you can forget about being a pantry chef in Åkarp. It's embarrassing for you to have a job like that when you could be doing this instead."

I was dreaming of Elsa again. The safety and the whole wheat scent. Her laugh and walk. The drool on her pillow as she slept. Once, she'd fallen asleep on an airplane, and when she woke up she noticed she'd been resting on the shoulder of the man next to her. It was soaked with her saliva. Typical Elsa, drooling on a fellow passenger in a completely irresistible way. That's how I thought of her now: Elsa light, Aniara dark. And then there was Lennart. Might he be out of the picture?

One night I decided to take the bull by the horns. I'd packed Aniara's things and put her bag by the door. I'd made the bed with Grandma's cherry-print bedspread, as well as the white crocheted piece that was supposed to lie on top of it. I had showered and shaved, put on a clean shirt, and done the dishes in the kitchen. As soon as she came through the door, I said:

"Aniara. It's over."

It took a moment before the tears came. She stormed around the entire house, stomping her heels. Then a new sound came from her chest, it was a humming at first, but soon it became more animalistic, like a scream. It turned into a scream. And then a roar.

She threw herself onto the bed. Tore off her clothes, the buttons flying off her blouse. I tried to get hold of her, calm her, and her eyes rolled back so that the whites faced me.

"Let's do it," she whispered.

I thought: One last time.

It must have been because I was so tense, torn up by the situation, but it was like she was cold inside. Her mouth, her sex. A great chill, a compact darkness, enveloped me.

Being inside her felt like being in a clamped jaw, pulling me into the cold, dark deep.

There was no orgasm. I couldn't. I could only taste my own tears, and I had to stop. I put on my pants and took her by the arm, led her to the door and threw her clothes out after her. She got dressed without looking at me. Then she left and closed the door behind her.

She returned the next day. Freshly washed and combed.

"The webcam. I forgot it yesterday. But it looks like we've set a viewer record."

I felt dizzy. I unmounted the camera and shut the door behind her.

I haven't seen her since then, except when she drives by or opens the door for a guest.

I've promised myself that I won't visit her web page, but some days I think I might, that I won't be able to resist. I'm like a stone, and Aniara, an abyss – the stone can only drop to the bottom. There is no other way, because it's not even a question of will. It's gravity.

Other days I think I can resist. And if only Lennart were to be kicked off the playing field, I could have Elsa back, and that cable inside me could be rewired and everything would be normal again. We'd enjoy our moments after we turned off the light, and laugh under the covers at her freshly baked scent.

Joshu says it's only a matter of time. Soon, I'll have forgotten both Aniara and Elsa, and then we'll go to Berlin. Have some fun. Screw around.

On the morning she was to plan her infidelity with Joan Roca, Jazmina Flores had dreamed that parts of her body were laid before her on a table, awaiting burial. Argancio Matas, her husband, had been sat across the table from her, placing her body parts in a coffin. In the dream, Jazmina Flores felt neither physical nor psychic pain. She even helped Argancio Matas fit the parts in the coffin, and when the coffin was full, she helped him seal it.

She said:

"But what are we going to do with the rest of me that isn't dead?"

"We'll have to add it when you die," said Argancio Matas, in the dream.

Jazmina Flores worried the dead parts would give off an unpleasant odor. She thought it was best they bury the coffin at once, and someone would just have to dig it up when the rest of her died.

She told Argancio Matas about the dream over breakfast.

"Argancio. I dreamed you were burying parts of me."

"The genitals?" asked Argancio Matas, looking up from his croissant.

"The genitals?" Jazmina Flores said.

"Yes. Was it the genitals that I was burying? Yours, in your dream?"

Jazmina Flores shook her head. She didn't remember whether it was her genitals that Argancio Matas had been burying in the dream.

"But you were cutting me into pieces, and I felt no pain."

"That can only mean one thing, Jazmina."

"What?"

"You're living inside a glass egg."

"Huh?"

"Well, you're confined, cocooned."

He opened his arms and continued:

"It's like this. If a cut doesn't hurt a person, then where does that person live but in a glass egg, if they're even alive at all. There's a question for you. Is that person even alive?"

Argancio Matas nodded to himself. He took a bite of his pastry and rolled it around in his mouth. Then he got up and put the cups on the dish rack. Jazmina Flores stayed at the table. Maybe Argancio Matas is right, she thought. Maybe Argancio Matas is right, and maybe Argancio Matas is wrong. If I had any self-esteem, I'd be able to tell. If I'd had a father, I'd be able to tell. If I'd had a father who had seen me, I would've become a different person, the kind who knows whether or not she's living inside a glass egg. Though, if I'd had a father I wouldn't have dreamed of being cut up.

These thoughts made her feel heavy and bloated. Thoughts were like smelly blankets – you had to keep them at a distance or their smell would rub off on you.

"Goodbye, Argancio Matas," she said. She took the lipstick out of her pocket, painted her lips, went down to the garage, backed her moped out, and made her way to her life-drawing class at Casón del Buen Retiro. There, she

148

undressed behind a screen and listened to the instructor introduce the course to the participants. It was an arts initiative supported by EU funds, intended to strengthen ties between Catalan and Castilian artists. Thirteen painters from Girona and Barcelona had been flown in to Madrid–Barajas, and there they were met by thirteen artists from Toledo, Madrid, and, of course, Cuenca, home to the Museum of Abstract Art, the reopening of which had caused quite a stir across Europe. The Castilian–Catalan palaver would now be over once and for all, or so the cabinet ministers thought. It was, they said, the first step in the right direction, toward reducing the astronomic expenditures caused by administrative nonsense in Spain's two metropolises.

Jazmina Flores modeled in the middle of the room. To her right were the Catalan artists, speaking Catalan, and to her left were the Castilian artists, speaking Castilian. Jazmina Flores didn't listen too closely. She was used to hearing soft voices mix with the sound of brushes on canvas. It was almost like a lullaby, and sometimes she was afraid she'd fall asleep and then they'd fire her. She wasn't indispensable, it had been pointed out. Jazmina Flores couldn't imagine having any other job. That's why she showed up on time and tried not to fall asleep during the sessions.

That morning, she thought about the things she wanted to have. It was a trick she'd picked up over the years: when she thought of something she wanted to have and imagined it was already hers, it pleased the artists. She knew it worked because in these moments the course leader would give her encouraging nods. A pair of shoes, for example. Today, she was thinking of a pair of calfskin shoes she'd seen at Hispanitas that cost eighty-six euros, a little more than her fee for the session. She felt almost giddy when one of the artists came up to her and whispered in her ear with a distinctly Catalan accent:

"Would you have anything against holding an apple?"

"Why?" Jazmina Flores wondered.

"It will be more decadent," the artist replied.

Jazmina Flores took the apple. It was large and round and red, and she thought of last night's dream. An image flickered, of Argancio Matas stowing something large and red in the coffin – was it her heart? She had just enough time to sniff the apple and notice it smelled of fall, or maybe even Christmas, before the same artist approached her again and stretched her arm forward, so she was holding the apple out and at an angle.

The teacher said:

"As you can see, Joan Roca has given the model an apple. It's a detail in his painting, of course, the rest of you don't have to paint it. You can look beyond the apple and just paint the body."

After a while the same artist said:

"I could use a snake, too."

There was, in fact, a stuffed python hidden away somewhere in the art school, and because that artist was a friend of Madrid's mayor, the teacher went above and beyond to find it. He called the caretaker, who went up to the box room on the third floor and rooted around among lampshades and Castilian dining tables painted black. After a while, he found it, carried it down the marble steps, and placed it on the bookshelf by Jazmina Flores' face.

Jazmina Flores looked the snake in the eye and offered it the apple.

"Excellent," said the artist from Barcelona. "Excellent."

*

The lesson ended at two o'clock. Jazmina Flores changed behind the screen. When she came out the room was empty except for the Catalan artist, who was standing at one end of the room, arms crossed, apparently waiting for her.

"Let me treat you to lunch," he said.

"I'm married," Jazmina Flores replied.

"I'm married, too," said the artist.

They stood in silence.

"I didn't ask if you wanted to marry me. Just if you wanted lunch."

That's some way he has about him, Jazmina Flores thought. It's exhausting. I see it every day at four o'clock in my Venezuelan telenovela, and now I have to endure it at my place of work. But it was the end of the month, and money was running out.

"Well, all right then," Jazmina Flores said, and walked down the stairs.

"My name is Joan Roca," the artist said when they reached the tulip garden.

"Jazmina Flores," Jazmina Flores said, reaching out her hand.

They took the small streets that ran between the Prado Museum and Sol. It was hot. A radio in the background reported that this was the hottest spring of the century, but the century had only just begun. They found a restaurant. A fan whirred in the corner. Joan Roca ordered a glass of white wine. Jazmina Flores ordered a beer and a Sprite, which she would mix together.

"Do you work there often?" Joan Roca wondered.

"A few days a week," Jazmina Flores said.

The waiter arrived with the glasses.

"So, what do you do?" Jazmina Flores said.

"I'm an architect. Maybe you've heard of me?"

"No."

Joan Roca took a drink.

"It's a good thing you haven't. People who've heard of me can be very ingratiating."

"Uh-huh," Jazmina Flores said.

"It's an 'emperor's new clothes' thing. People want to be around me, without really knowing why."

"Uh-huh," Jazmina Flores said.

"But let's not talk about that now," Joan Roca said. "Let's create a bubble for you and me, where only we exist and no one else can enter."

"Yes," said Jazmina Flores, and checked the time.

"And now I'd like to tell you about the suite I'm currently painting," said Joan Roca.

"Uh-huh?"

"Yes. This suite is called 'Eve.'"

The food arrived. Jazmina Flores had ordered chorizo in cider and Joan Roca a steak of wild boar. They ate in silence. Jazmina Flores now thought the chorizo had been a bad idea – she'd be gassy all afternoon.

"The problem is," Joan Roca said, chewing, "I don't have anyone to pose for me. I mean, everyone knows who I am, and you can see it in them. I need someone like you. Someone more unworldly, sequestered, who doesn't get that sparkle in her eyes when she sees me. And I think today went great. With the snake and the apple. Work with me. What do you say?"

Jazmina Flores chewed. She thought of Argancio Matas, and then she thought of her aunt, who liked her to visit a few times a week. The artist lived in Barcelona. How would that go?

"I don't know," she said. "There's a lot to consider."

"Think about it," the artist said. "I pay well."

*

For dessert, Jazmina ordered lemon sorbet, hoping it would coat the gassy chorizo like a soothing membrane. Joan Roca ordered coffee with a big shot of Orujo.

"I don't know what's happening inside me right now," said Joan Roca when he'd finished the coffee. "But your presence is doing something to me. Maybe it's your perfume. What perfume are you wearing?"

"LouLou."

"LouLou? That's awfully cheap!"

"Is it? I didn't think it was that cheap."

"No, I don't mean it like that. The smell is sordid, sweet."

"Uh-huh," said Jazmina Flores.

"Do you mean that blue bottle? With the red edge?"

"Yes. Sort of a plastic blue."

"Yes, yes. Yes, you really are an Eve. Now I think about it, that's precisely the perfume you should wear, and I'm not saying this to insult you. I'm reevaluating the perfume now I know you wear it. LouLou – of course! What other perfume would Eve be wearing? I told you – you're perfect!"

Joan Roca wiped his nose with the napkin. Jazmina Flores looked at the clock.

"We have to go now," she said. "I'll get fired if I'm late."

They walked down Calle Huertas, past Champagnería Gala and the Prado's tapas bar. When they came out on Paseo del Prado, exhaust fumes hit them, but today the general stink of filth was mixed with other, more exotic scents from the Botanical Garden.

"I had such a strange dream last night," Joan Roca said.

"Is that so?" said Jazmina Flores.

"Yes. Strange, and quite awful."

"Is that so?"

"You want to hear?"

"Yes."

"But it feels like I'm the one doing all the talking. Don't you think it feels that way? Like I'm doing all the talking?"

"No," said Jazmina Flores. "I'm not that talkative."

"Well then, OK. But you're doing fine? The food was quite good?"

"It was."

"Maybe it's too hot."

"Yes, that would be the only thing," said Jazmina Flores.

"OK, well if you're doing fine, I'll tell you about the dream."

Joan Roca slowed his pace.

"So, you see, Jazmina, I dreamed I saw a married couple in front of a coffin."

"Uh-huh."

"Yes, and the man was stuffing the woman into the coffin. In pieces. She was lying in front of him, cut into pieces. Can you imagine. And he was stuffing one piece after the next into a coffin, and he seemed to be completely unaffected."

"The genitals?" Jazmina Flores said and swallowed.

"The genitals?"

"Yes. Was it the genitals he was stuffing into the coffin? The husband. Of that woman, in your dream."

"I don't know," Joan Roca replied. "But I don't think so. I would have noticed if it was."

They'd arrived at the Botanical Garden's gate. The tulips in the beds at the entrance were bright red and yellow. Jazmina Flores thought it looked like they were in flames.

"The funny thing was," Joan Roca continued, "you couldn't sense any strong emotions in the dream. It all seemed plastic-wrapped, somehow, as though she'd calmly allowed herself to be maimed. And I was struck by the thought that . . . "

"Yes?"

"Maybe that's what we do. With other people, I mean. Maybe we maim each other, and well, if that's true, then it is, of course . . . "

The sentence hung in the air. Jazmina Flores kept looking at the tulips.

"I don't know," she said. "There are practical reasons for allowing yourself to be maimed. It's cheaper to split the rent."

Joan Roca looked up.

"You *are* a funny one, Jazmina Flores! I thought so from the start – you should be exhibited. I'm standing here wallowing in an idiotic dream, and you are just so simple. So undamaged, in a way. I must see you again. Can we say we'll return to this bubble after your session? We'll go to Retiro, I'll buy a bottle of fizz and then we'll just be."

"Be?"

"Yes. Be. Are you in?"

"I don't know. I should go visit my aunt."

"Please."

"I don't know."

"Please."

"OK, fine."

He isn't my type, Jazmina Flores thought during the afternoon session. Sure, he's still tall and handsome, but still, not my type. Anyway, I'm married. Her head felt tired. It was spring, she thought. Sunshine, smells, tension in her neck from eating lunch with a man she didn't know, who wanted her to work for him. The gases in her stomach expanded and made strange sounds. She hoped the instructor wouldn't hear, or the artists.

She tried to imagine the shoes she'd seen earlier. During the morning session, before the snake and apple had come into the picture, she'd thought she'd swing by Goya when the afternoon session finished. Give in to temptation, which would have been nice, would have allowed her to feel like she'd actually made something of the day. But now she couldn't concentrate on the shoes. She saw the Catalan architect's face in front of her and felt nervous when she thought about being with him on the lawn in Retiro.

"Chin up, Jazmina," the instructor said.

Jazmina Flores raised her chin. The brushes scraped the canvases. The din of city traffic came through the open window.

"That's it for today," the instructor said. "We hope you've had a nice day here in Madrid. For my part, I'm grateful to have spent this time with you and to watch the relationship between Spain's two metropolises grow increasingly cordial. It really is encouraging!"

The artists put their brushes in the jars by their easels. The Castilian artists went back to speaking Castilian with their colleagues, and the Catalans in Catalan with theirs.

Joan Roca approached Jazmina Flores.

"You haven't forgotten about Retiro, have you?" he whispered.

"I haven't."

"I'll wait for you down there, I just have to run out and buy the fizz. By the tulips in ten minutes, OK?"

Jazmina Flores dressed behind the screen, and the teacher paid her seventy-nine euros.

"Here you go," he said. "We'll forget about invoicing, it makes things so expensive. VAT and all that."

Jazmina Flores said thank you and walked down the stairs.

Retiro was full of people. On the lawns, English and Scandinavian tourists sunbathed. On the asphalt paths, Spanish and South American children ran around among large Disney characters who spoke with Peruvian accents. There was a balloon seller and a gypsy woman carrying rosemary, looking for women with plunging necklines she could slip a sprig into, hoping to prick them and stick them with a payment.

"What a nice day," Jazmina Flores said.

"Yes," said Joan Roca.

They lay in the shade of a chestnut tree. Joan Roca opened the bottle and filled the plastic flutes. They people-watched and drank the cava in silence.

When Jazmina Flores had finished her first glass, she lay down and looked up into the trees. They were spinning, she thought. It was of course the effect of the cava – she and Argancio Matas never drank cava at home.

"I'm dizzy," she said.

"From that little glass?"

"Yes. I never drink cava."

"What kind of husband doesn't give you cava? That's rule number one: always make sure women have wine."

Joan Roca set his glass aside and lay down, resting his head against one of the roots.

"Tell me more about you," he said. "About you and your husband."

"There isn't much to say."

"Come on. There always is."

"I don't know what to say."

"What does he do?"

"He works for a company off the eastbound highway."

"What does he do there?"

"Makes dots."

"Makes dots?"

"Yes. Diagrams."

"You're really not a talkative one, are you?" Joan Roca said.

"No," replied Jazmina Flores.

"But we don't need to talk much. It's OK to just lie here. I'm lying here thinking about my Eve suite, and hoping you'll agree to come work with me. And I'm thinking it would be nice if you came a little closer. Like this? Can I lie like this? You're probably lying there thinking your thoughts, too. What are you thinking?"

"I was actually thinking about when I was a child."

"Were you?"

"Yes, I was just reminded of something. It has to do with the light I think. I always think about what happened with my mother when the light is like this."

"Why?"

"Because the light was like this when my mother told my stepfather I wasn't his child."

"Sounds dramatic."

"It was. My mother had sworn, as you do, that if the sun peeked out of the clouds at a certain moment, she would tell him I wasn't his child. Then it happened. The sun came out. She got scared and told him."

"What happened next?"

"My mother said my father would come. My real father, that is."

"And who was he?"

"I don't know. I've never met him. But my mother met him, just once, in the blue grotto on our island. He was from the mainland. Tall and handsome. A wonderful man, my mother said."

"What is your mother's name?"

"Gilda Flores. After what happened with my stepfather, my mother began waiting at the harbor every Sunday. She said she'd written to him and that he'd promised to come pick us up one Sunday. We would put on our best clothes and stand there, waiting for my real father. Waiting and waiting."

"So you'd stand and wait at the harbor?"

"Every Sunday. Her hand would be clamped around mine. We'd stand at the edge. On the bench behind us, a group of island women would sit, knitting. All you could hear was the waves breaking against the boats and the sound of their knitting needles. The women would stare at our backs, thinking my mother had made everything up."

"Did he come?"

"No. He never came. And one night, my stepfather got drunk down at the bar and came home and grabbed my mother by the hair and dragged her up to the top of Cala Inferno. I ran alongside, begging him to stop, but he was so drunk and angry it was like his eyes were going to pop out of his head. Then he threw my mother off the cliff."

"Did she die?"

"Well, of course she died."

Joan Roca said nothing. His expression was grim. Jazmina Flores sighed. So now his mood had changed, just when the cava had begun to make her feel elated for the first time that day! She looked up at the tree and thought its crown was spinning quickly, now. And then she sat up and helped herself to more cava. Joan Roca had moved away from her.

"All OK, Joan?" she asked.

"All OK, Jazmina. What year did you say you were born?"
She said the year and he turned away again.

Jazmina Flores lay back down and looked up at the tree. She thought about the dream Joan Roca had recounted over lunch, which must've been the same one she'd dreamed. She glanced at him. He lay outstretched with his eyes shut, his blazer folded into a pillow. He was quite beautiful. Graceful, in a way. And he had very dark hair and bushy eyebrows, like Dalí. Maybe she should give in to his advances. She smiled to herself and thought that maybe this right here was happiness, plain and simple, lying like this and waiting to be kissed. And while she was waiting, she drifted off to sleep, and her sleep was snug and safe, like warm cotton.

A child's cries woke her. She sat up. The sun had slipped behind the clouds, and Joan Roca was gone.

She saw the chestnut tree, the empty bottle, and, in the distance, the crying child, chasing after a balloon that was floating higher and higher up into the sky.

NOTHING HAS CHANGED

Everything was the same back then, too, but in a different way. We lived in an apartment on the street that runs from Kulturen up toward Lundagård. Me and Klara. The kitchen was a decent size, facing the street, and we took turns cooking dinner. On the fridge we kept a shopping list: toilet paper, cottage cheese, brown rice, olive oil, wine for the weekend. We came and went as we pleased, and our place was pretty messy. The bathroom was newly renovated and had a blue plastic floor and a tub. I did take baths in there, but thinking back on it, I can't actually remember bathing in that tub. The main door said "Palmström," which was Klara's last name. My last name wasn't up there. We kept putting it off and just never got around to it. I had the big bedroom, she the small one. Both faced the courtyard. We never brought boyfriends home. It wasn't an agreement between us, it just turned out that way. Klara's mattress was on the floor, and I had a bed. I didn't wear pajamas and had no curtains. Klara might not have worn pajamas either. She didn't have any curtains.

We had it pretty good, Klara and me, until the incident with the nameplate.

*

We spent the summers with our respective families. Klara's family would rent a house on an island off the coast of Italy; mine went to the summerhouse in Blekinge. One summer, on the day we were due to leave, there was a large hairy spider in the bathroom. Klara had already gone and I was just grabbing my toothbrush when I saw it. It was on the floor. Not moving. I got scared. Silly, I know, but I did. I thought I should try to overcome my fear and set it free in the courtyard, so I fetched a glass from the kitchen. When I returned it still hadn't moved. I put the glass over it and left to get a postcard to slide under it, so I could carry it out. When I slid the postcard under, the spider went insane and started running around the inside of the glass. "Bonkers," my brother would've said. Disgusting, I thought, and then the phone rang. It was Dad. He said he'd been standing on the street for nearly twenty minutes. Could I please get a move on? I took my bag, checked that the stove was off, and locked the upper and lower locks.

A few weeks later, fall term began. We were back in the apartment, living our own lives. The first months of term were laid-back, as usual. We sat with our books under the beech trees in Lundagård, looking at people, smoking the occasional joint. One weekend, we took the boat to Copenhagen, ate ice cream with chocolate mallow cups mixed in and drank beer, our legs dangling over the Nyhavn dock. One day, a letter fell through the mail slot. *Miss Palmström*, it read on the envelope, and it was signed by someone called Markus. He lived across the courtyard. He wrote that he could see Miss Palmström taking off her clothes at night, before she went to bed. It had begun by chance. Then he'd made a habit of waiting at the window each night with the light off, looking out across the courtyard. So many nights had now gone by, and he'd seen her so many times, he thought he'd fallen in love. Now he wanted to meet her.

Klara held it up.

"Check this out," she said. "I have a secret admirer."

I read it. The tone was ridiculous and it was full of spelling mistakes. I thought there had to be something wrong with a person for them to send a letter like that. Calling someone "Miss," I mean, what century is this?

"How do you know he's *your* admirer?" I said.

"'Cos it says. Palmström, that's me."

"But he doesn't know that. It could just as well be me. My last name isn't on the door. My room faces the courtyard, too."

"Same difference," Klara said. "He can't even spell. Neither of us will be into him anyway."

Klara was in a relationship with her psychologist. First they did therapy, then they did each other. Sick, I thought, and I tried to avoid talking about him. Klara had always liked older, cultivated men. The psychologist was perfect for her, she thought, but I still found it sick. I was with Konrad, a guy who studied law, just like I did. His diplomat parents hosted parties in their garden. We used to get drunk at the student union and have sex all over the place. Sometimes we studied, but Konrad didn't have a good head for it. Sometimes we helped each other during exams. Passed notes. Once, we had sex in the exam room toilet and got kicked out and both failed. But Konrad's dad talked to the prefect, so we were allowed to retake the test in a classroom at the law school. We sat alone, unsupervised, and wrote down all the same answers to the questions. We both got the highest grade. Konrad also thought it was sick that

Klara was having sex with her psychologist. But maybe he was just jealous because he wasn't old and cultivated and graying at the temples.

After a few days, another letter from Markus arrived. Say where and when, it said. Give me a chance. Just one chance. I have to meet you.

"I have to go," Klara said. "I have to at least let him talk to me."

"But what if he thinks he's writing to me?" I asked her again.

"He's probably writing to me," Klara said. "I usually get undressed by the window before I get into bed."

"So do I," I said.

We looked at each other. We tried to laugh it off. Klara made tea. We drank and talked about the psychologist and Konrad. Markus's letter sat between us on the table.

Klara and I used to exercise together. Klara weighed less than I did, but I was taller. Klara had short blond hair, mine was long and dark. We were quite different. I was coordinated, she could run fast. We would do face masks and hair treatments at the sauna. We would take walks, and the wind would make Klara happy; she said it made her feel alive. Alive if she was in a good mood, angry if she was in a bad mood. One day, Klara brought home a fasting kit from the health food store on Mårtenstorget. She wanted us to fast.

"It's a conscious choice," she said. "Let's get rid of that extra weight once and for all. We can do this."

We drank prune juice for breakfast, tomato juice for lunch. I had to pee all the time and my head ached and I couldn't sleep.

"Drink more water," said Klara.

We still drank herbal tea in the kitchen, though we didn't talk as long as usual because we were both tired all the time. The psychologist called and praised Klara's discipline. I listened through the door, and then told Klara I thought the psychologist was a lech. Klara told me to mind my own business. If I wanted to have a floppy puppy like Konrad, that was my choice. I said Konrad was neither married nor my psychologist.

"He's probably not the psychologist type," said Klara. "He's a philistine."

I thought: A philistine isn't the opposite of a psychologist, but then again maybe I was confusing it all. I might not have been thinking clearly anymore, on account of the fast. I said we shouldn't fight when we were fasting. We had to ration our energy. We went to our rooms and studied. Klara was studying theoretical physics and me law, but I've already said that. That night, Konrad called.

"I'm outside on the street," he said. "Want to come down?"

"I'm fasting," I said. "I'm pooped."

After a while, there was a knock on the door. I thought it might be Markus, was curious and wanted to open up. But Klara had already run to the door and was unlocking it. It was Konrad. He'd brought pizza capricciosa and brownies. Coca-Cola. We set the table, and I don't think any food has ever tasted so good. I ate it all up. Klara had taken her herbal tea to the dining room, saying she couldn't handle the pizza smell, it smelled like greasy pig. After dinner, I burped. Konrad laughed.

Then he said:

"Some discipline that friend of yours has."

"Discipline's one word for it," I said. "She's not thinking twice about getting off with her psychologist, who's old and married."

"Yeah," said Konrad. "But still. It still takes discipline."

"Oh come the fuck on," I said, suddenly feeling bloated. I'd read somewhere that if you deplete your fat deposits and then fill them up again, the body will replenish every ounce of fat. That was probably what was happening to me. I heard Klara set her teacup down on the table in the dining room.

"Hey Konrad," I said. "How about putting my name up on the door?"

We took the letters out of the toolbox in the cleaning closet. Konrad slid off the glass and fiddled them into place. *Palmström Blomberg*, the door now read. Konrad sat on the floor, trying to slide the glass back into place. It seemed to have broken. Then I heard the door from the courtyard open. Steps on the stairs. Then there was a guy holding three red roses, with wet-combed hair and jeans. A trace of mustache. Smelling of cologne. He stopped and looked at me, then at Konrad. He was about to turn and go when Klara arrived.

"Hi," she said. "Markus? I'm Klara. Klara Palmström."

He looked back at me, and then at Konrad. I could swear he didn't understand a thing. Klara said:

"That's Ania. Ania Blomberg and her boyfriend Konrad."

"I see," Markus said, and handed the roses to Klara.

Klara invited Markus in for coffee in our kitchen. After a few days, she took her things and moved in with him across the courtyard. She was tired of the psychologist, said he was too Freudian for her, she'd been developing a preference for Jung. Markus was a nice man when it came down to it. Maybe not the world's most cultivated, but good and solid, you know.

*

About the spider. When I came back from vacation that summer I found it under the glass. It was dead. It had gotten thinner, if you can say that about a spider. It was thin, with long legs and a tiny spot in the center of its abdomen. It had simply wasted away. I scolded myself for forgetting it and wondered how many laps the spider had run round the inside of the glass before it died. I wondered if it had suffocated or starved. I wondered a lot of strange things, as usual. I normally try to push away thoughts like that. The spider had died and it was my fault, and there wasn't anything else to it. But every time I went into the bathroom I saw it in front of me. Wasting away, running circles in the glass.

Konrad moved his things into Klara's room. His synth, his golf clubs, and his wet suit. They're there now, along with my boxes of old books, photos, a few paintings. We have a shopping list on the fridge: bacon, shaving cream, sour milk. In the evenings we watch TV, sometimes we study. Sometimes we meet up with Markus and Klara, and Markus and I sneak looks at each other.

I wish I could say I still undress the way I used to, while Konrad brushes his teeth. That I still don't have any curtains, still don't wear pajamas to bed. That Marcus still stands there looking at me from his darkened window across the courtyard while Klara brushes her teeth in the bathroom. But that's not how it is. Coupledom has changed Konrad and me. I wear washed-out flannel pajamas and he wears a brown tracksuit from Stadium. We fall asleep in front of the TV almost every night, and Konrad's mom hung us green-striped curtains in the bedroom. To say that

Markus and I sneak looks at each other is an overstatement. Actually, we check each other out openly, from head to toe, sizing each other up and wondering how much the other earns. Klara and I size each other up the same way, searching for signs of excess weight. Konrad and I have stopped having sex everywhere. Sometimes we have sex in bed, behind the green-striped curtains. Sometimes I feel like rebelling. Screaming. Packing a bag and going far, far away. Sometimes I say things without thinking.

Like when we all had dinner the other day, and I drank too much red wine. I was going on and on and Konrad got up to dish some more food. In the candlelight, I suddenly found the three of them so beautiful. Still so young, a gleam in their eyes from the wine. Then there was something more, something strange, I don't know. I said:

"It's kind of a drag, all this couple stuff. Don't you think?"

They squirmed.

"It is what you make of it," said Markus.

Konrad nodded in agreement. Klara fingered the base of her wine glass.

"It's cozy," Klara said. "Safe. Homey. You, like, know what you're getting."

We sat in silence, Konrad poured more wine.

Then I said it:

"Maybe we should have an orgy? All four of us. Liven things up a bit."

They looked at me. Klara's mascara had run and Markus was smiling skeptically, his wet-combed hair slightly rumpled.

"You're joking," Markus said.

I looked at Konrad. He was leaning against the wall, picking at the label on the wine bottle.

"The things you come up with," he said.

Klara got up and flicked the switch, flooding the table with light. Konrad blew out the candles.

We went back to our dinner. Roast beef, potatoes au gratin, and red wine. Food in our mouths, jaws grinding.

"You're among friends," Klara said eventually. "So don't worry. Nothing has changed."

She came out as I was putting a roof on the woodshed. She was wearing her black turtleneck and coughing.

"I have to tell you something," she said. "I've been unfaithful."

I raised my eyebrows. We'd never asked each other any questions. Never talked about what we could or could not do. What a strange thing, to come out into the rain and tell me.

"You're going to catch cold," I said. "Go inside and we'll talk about it later."

She shook her head.

"You have to come down. He's here. In the living room."

"Who?"

"The man I was unfaithful with is sitting inside."

We went in and yes, indeed, there he was.

He was young. At least fifteen years younger than Hanna. He sat with his legs spread wide and was wearing a black hoodie. One ear was studded with earrings from the earlobe all the way to the top. A muscular guy. I wondered if he'd come here to make a scene. Good thing Daisy was at a friend's. He must have come unannounced, because Hanna's paintings were scattered all over the living room.

She'd only been painting for a few months. Large, dark paintings, paintings without any finesse. Masts reaching for the heavens. I'd tell her that those masts would break off at the first storm, snap like splinters and end up as driftwood. Now he was sitting there, the man she'd betrayed me with, surrounded by her boat masts and unfinished sunsets.

"Hi," he said.

"Hi," I said.

"I'm sorry. Really, I didn't want to intrude. But I had nowhere else to go."

He got up and came toward me with an outstretched hand. Now I could see he was tall and graceful, with a body like a dancer's. We shook hands, a quick squeeze, and then tried to focus on something else.

"The masts are sprawling," he said to Hanna. "It looks like they're going to tip those boats over."

"Kent thinks so, too," said Hanna.

The guy nodded and shoved his hands in his pockets.

"I still don't quite understand," I said, clearing my throat. "Are you planning on staying with us?"

"Only for a while," he said. "Until I've figured things out with my girlfriend."

I needed to be alone. So I put my boots on and went back out into the rain.

As I laid the roof, I thought: This kind of thing happens in long relationships. You live an entire life together, you can't expect everything to be perfect all the time. You have to be there, show up for it. Treat people the way you'd want them to treat you. That might sound like a dumb rule, but I've always thought it was a good one. Now I was thinking about it again. I was thinking: I will treat Hanna the way I would want her to treat me in this situation.

Because, of course, I've had my share of fun, even if I was clever enough to choose people who didn't show up on my doorstep asking to move in. Maybe it was a question of luck. But there had been something going on with her lately. I couldn't quite put my finger on it, but things hadn't been the same. I'd noticed the change around her birthday. She was thirty-nine years old now, she'd said, and a better person. I'd wondered what it was about turning thirty-nine that made you a better person. Then she said she cried more often, and had started painting bigger boats. When you cried you were open, and the bigger the boat, the smaller the horizon. The empty surface of the sea had less space, and that meant that you'd learned to avoid emptiness. I'd been looking at her differently since she'd talked about the surface of the sea like that, like a person aware of their own flaws looking at what might well be a decent person. Now it was clear that this newly won decency hadn't stopped her from helping herself to someone else's chocolate box. Or offering someone else a chocolate from mine, for that matter.

After a while I went back inside, and the guy was gone. I asked Hanna where to, and she said she didn't know, but he'd left his backpack so he was probably coming back. Things were tense between us. She went into the kitchen to cook, and I sat down and watched TV. We ate when Daisy came home from her friend's, and that wasn't the time to talk about what had happened, either. I thought I should probably get to the bottom of this with her and kick him to the curb. But I did neither of these things. I pictured what would happen if she actually packed her bags and left. Pictured her standing at the bus stop in her raincoat, with that guy by her side. I wasn't ready for anything like that. I said to myself: It's a confusing situation. Sleep on it, and you'll know what to do as soon as you wake up.

When I came downstairs the next morning, he was at the breakfast table talking to Daisy. Hanna had set out coffee cups for us both and was moving uneasily between the table, the refrigerator, and the kitchen counter. Daisy kept talking, whipping her Sindy doll in the air, and she seemed to like him. Lukas was his name, by the way. Then Daisy wanted to show him her room, and he followed her, tall and graceful, through the living room. Hanna poured herself a cup and sat across from me.

"How's it going?" she said.

"It's OK," I said.

"What a mess, huh?"

"It's fine. It's not your fault he's intruding."

She smiled gratefully.

"I suppose I should apologize," she said. "But you can see it's not serious. He's only twenty."

I nodded.

"Once is as good as never."

"Thank you," she said, and squeezed my hand.

Daisy and Lukas came back. Hanna told Daisy it was time to go to school. "When are you leaving?" Hannah asked Lukas. When are you leaving? It would've been more like her to ask: "How long were you thinking of staying?" I drank my coffee, which was lukewarm.

"What are you studying?" I asked Lukas.

"Philosophy," he said.

"Ah," I said. "It's not every day you meet someone who works out *and* studies philosophy."

"You don't have to ignore your looks just because you're busy cultivating your own garden," Lukas said.

I buttered my bread and didn't say anything else. Lukas and Hanna talked about what was in the paper, agreeing there wasn't ever really anything special in there. When he talked to her, his voice sounded different to when he spoke with me. In fact, he always spoke with a special feeling that's hard to explain. It was both naive and earnest, and when he addressed Hanna there was an extra warmth to his voice. Sitting there, listening to him, I thought about what my sister had said after reading a book about men and women.

"You men are dumb fuckers," she'd said. "It's a wonder you manage to survive as a species."

She'd been waving her hands around and then her chubby fingers grabbed the book's spine. I didn't take her very seriously, because my sister always dove in head-first and believed what she was told, but she was quick to redeem herself. Yet what she said was still ringing in my ears: Some men can go for decades without noticing anything's wrong.

"Men," she said, "think everything is fine and dandy, and then one day the wife finds someone else and bails. When they talk about it later, the wife will say I've had the most boring time with you. Fifteen monotonous years, she'll say. But why didn't you say anything, the man replies. I did say, I said it all the time, she counters. Then the man has a vague memory of something. A dull nagging in the back of his skull. About travel and books and other kinds of lives. Going to the theater and being in book clubs. And only then does he realize her comments were directed at him."

I wondered if Hanna had ever thought she was having the most boring time with me.

*

That same night, Lukas made pizza. He'd gone to the liquor store and bought beer for him and me and red wine for Hanna. You could smell his pizza baking throughout the house. The kitchen was covered in trays of rising dough, and the floor was dusted with flour. The beer was cold and good, and he made eye contact and wore a pleasant expression. When we talked about my job, he said he'd always been interested in the felling of trees. As a child he'd watched his grandfather, how he used to chop a wedge into a trunk and then fell the tree so it landed right where he wanted. It was one of his best childhood memories, his grandfather's patient tree felling. I wanted to say there was no art to it. But I also knew to be careful with people's childhood memories, because those memories are not rational and cannot be challenged.

"How about you give it a try?" I said. "Tomorrow I'll bring the truck, and we'll go cut down a few trees in the yard. There's an old birch or two that could do with coming down before the winter storms."

Lukas said if there was one thing in life he wanted to try, it was felling a tree by remote control. You don't have to be boring just because you study philosophy, he added, and we laughed. Then we sat on the sofa and watched whatever was on TV. It was a movie with a couple driving in a car, and the woman's mom and some Mafia guy were chasing them. They checked into a motel and the woman, who was pregnant, vomited on the floor, and then there was a pretty special scene with that vomit and the flies zipping around it. Lukas knew all the actors' names. Hanna nodded and seemed to be really into the movie.

*

175

Lukas came with me the next morning, and the one after that. After he'd stayed a whole week, I'd almost forgotten he'd been Hanna's lover. I saw him more as a buddy or relative. I liked having him in the truck. I needed the help, and I enjoyed talking to him. No complaining, just good conversation and steady, solid work. Soon he was almost as good as I was at felling trees. He even thought it was fun, didn't seem to lose any of his initial enthusiasm and give in to the routine and monotony, and that meant I managed to keep those things at bay too. When we were driving between jobs he sometimes talked about philosophers. Especially Schopenhauer. He said Schopenhauer had said all of nature was one big torture chamber. Everyone was suffering like hell, the whole earth was crawling with suffering. Maybe even the plants were suffering.

"Imagine a living tree," he said once, "and there you come, with your claw, taking it in your cold grip and sliding the blade through."

I was with him, to an extent. I too could sympathize with a worm being hooked. But when he went on about the trees, that was overkill.

"You sound like a vegan," I said. "Soon you'll be talking about those poor pigs, too."

We drove home in silence that day, and I thought: Enough is enough. I'd been handed this strange life I hadn't asked for. I was making a friend I couldn't tell my colleagues about. If someone stopped by, we told them Lukas was a friend of the family. It was a strange situation that couldn't last forever.

"Enough is enough," I said at the dinner table. "I know you didn't want to intrude, and it's been nice having you here, but now you have to respect our privacy and pack your bags."

The table fell silent. I kept quiet, too, but sometimes you have to say what needs to be said. Then you have to take what comes your way, and often it's not as bad as you think.

Though Lukas made no move to pack his bag, it seemed like my prayers had been answered. The very next night there was a knock at the door, and there was his girlfriend, Angelica, in jeans and a leather jacket. She had skinny legs and long, messy hair.

"I heard Lukas is living here," she said.

"Yes, this is where he's been staying," I replied. "Temporarily."

"I'm here to talk to him."

"Come on in," I said.

Lukas was in the living room watching TV. When he saw Angelica, he jumped out of the couch, went up to her, and gave her a hug. She shrank.

"Hold up," she said. "I have a thing or two to say first."

"OK," he said. "Say it."

"If you act like an idiot one more time I'll kill you."

"OK," Lukas said. "Anything else?"

"Yes. One more thing. Remember that girl you cheated on me with."

"Yes."

"Do you also remember saying you'd piss on her for me?"

"Yes."

"I want you to."

"What?"

"I've been thinking about it a lot. I'm going to give you another chance, but it'll be your last one. I'll come with you. We'll go over to see the girl and you'll piss on her for me, and then we're even."

Angelica blew a bubble. I could smell her raspberry-flavored gum from across the room. At that moment, Hanna came in, carrying one of her mast paintings.

"Hi," Hanna said, and reached out her hand. "I'm Hanna. And who are you?"

Angelica gave Hanna a dark look and refused her hand.

"That's Angelica," said Lukas. "You know. Angelica. My girlfriend."

"Is that so," Hanna said, and set the painting on the floor.

"How do you know each other?" Angelica said, narrowing her eyes at Hanna.

"That's Hanna," Lukas said, eyes flitting.

"And who's Hanna, moron?"

When he didn't reply, she said:

"Come on, who are you living with? Who's the old lady? Who's the old man?"

"They're . . . "

Beads of sweat were forming at his hairline.

"Well. They're my aunt and uncle," he said. "Kent and Hanna. Have I never mentioned them?"

"Maybe. So, Uncle Kent and Aunt Hanna. Is that right. Quite the couple. Come on now, you've got some pissing to do, remember?"

They went out the door. Hanna and I stayed in the hall.

I don't know who got pissed on on Angelica's behalf, or if Lukas managed to talk himself out of it, but the ice between them must have thawed somehow, because after a few hours they came back in a markedly better mood. They'd bought frozen pizzas at the grocery store, and they baked them in the oven. They treated the place like their own. Meanwhile Daisy, Hanna, and I sat in the living room watching TV.

"This is getting to be a bit much," I said.

"Yes," Hanna said.

After a while she said:

"Lukas is a fine boy. It's too bad he lets Angelica push him around."

As she spoke, she looked genuinely sad. I wanted to hug her, but the thought of comforting her about this made me feel stupid. How much of a pushover can you be? I made sure to keep some distance between us, but I did understand what she'd seen in him. I mean, as much as you can understand in that situation. He was good at living; it was that simple. He could whip up a pizza at the right moment, grab some beers from the fridge when needed. Make eye contact and fell a tree like a man. Then there was his way of talking, getting into things. Even if it was stuff like the lawn being a torture chamber, it was a particular way of looking at reality, and he stood by it. He breathed conviction, or maybe it was his youth. Maybe we'd been like that once, too – naive, full of conviction, enthusiastic – but that was a long time ago now. We'd slid into something else, something that made us feel we were cut from a different cloth when we were with a person like Lukas. Sure, it was out of line for Hanna to have jumped into bed with him. She should've taken on a different role, a more honorable role, like a protective friend – or why not something decadent, like that woman in *Dangerous Liaisons*. She could've suggested he live with us for free or something, and then we could've both enjoyed his company. But this. Well, well. I don't know. I wasn't moralizing about her; she'd never moralized about me. I just sat there and watched the quiz show while Lukas and Angelica made a ruckus in the kitchen.

Around the time Daisy went to bed, they came in to us, and Lukas's backpack was slung over his shoulder.

"Later," he said. "Thanks for everything."

He waved and left. Hanna and I stayed on the sofa. I took her hand. It was cold. She looked pale. It was flu season. I fetched a bottle of wine from the cellar. "Finally, something to celebrate," I said. She didn't say anything, but drank a lot and got tipsy. We went to the kitchen, made roast beef sandwiches with dried onions, cleared away the scattering of stale pizza crusts. Then we went to bed. When we woke up the next morning, it felt like we were on our honeymoon. It was luxurious, us, all by ourselves: her and me and Daisy. I bought buns from the bakery. We took a walk by the sea. I suggested we take a trip. Barcelona or Rome, Dublin maybe.

NUESTRA SEÑORA DE LA ASUNCIÓN

Once, I met a writer who said he couldn't bear to be a writer anymore. It was at a party in Madrid, and I don't remember how I ended up there but it was on Calle Ventura de la Vega, so I assume someone I'd met that night had taken me along (my own friends, to the extent that I even had any, lived in completely different places). "If you really are a writer you can't stop just like that," I said. "I have to," he replied. "Because I feel myself gravitating toward madness, and the days I'm not gravitating toward madness, I gravitate toward something even worse." "What?" I asked. He said he didn't know, but he had his wife and child to think of, and as far as madness went, he believed, like Roberto Bolaño, that it was contagious.

I didn't go out much at the time. I was newly married and my Spanish was bad. My son was about a year old, and I was always home – except every now and then, when my husband would return from his travels, put his bags down in the hall, and look at me, sat on the sofa after days spent glued to soap operas. I used to toss the caramel wrappers right on the floor, and I'd put my empty soda cans in the bookshelf behind the sofa. The gum went in the flowerpot on the floor. I must have looked bloated and envious there on the sofa when my husband came home. He always wore a tie and a glossy suit, and when he stood there with his coal-black Spanish hair it was as if you could see all the world's airports in his eyes. But he never commented on the mess or said I looked like someone who hadn't washed her hair in a week. He would say: "Now it's your turn to go out." And he'd pick up our son, who'd start screaming. Our son would vomit big yellow smears on his suit, but he'd just laugh and look happy. Spaniards love children. They are well dressed and laid-back; I've always liked the combination.

Because I so rarely went out, I sometimes thought I'd forgotten how to talk to people. How typical that the first person I met at the party was a writer who didn't want to be a writer, I thought. I sit at home for weeks, maybe months, and when I finally get out and have a conversation, it's with a writer who thinks he's going mad. After the madness thing, he said, he craved completely unbridled sex. *Tengo ganas de sexo desenfrenado*, he said. *Estoy más salida que el pico de una mesa*, he added, and exactly what that meant I didn't understand at the time. When he asked where I was from, I said France. Why did I say that? Possibly because people in Latin countries don't really take you seriously when you say you're from Sweden. Or so that he, in his state, wouldn't confuse me with someone who might have swum topless in Benidorm in the Eighties.

I kept mingling. The next person I spoke with was a woman who introduced herself as Filomena. "This is a party for people who have problems," she said. "No one here is normal except you, and you're not even from Spain." I asked what she did, and she said her husband owned a bar. I told her about the writer I'd just talked to and she said she knew him, at this party almost everyone knew each other, and tomorrow they were all going to Granada together on a bus. This was just a pre-party, or not a pre-party but a kind of run-up. "A bus all the way to Granada?" I said, and she nodded. Later, she asked for my number.

It was four in the morning when I got home to the apartment on Calle Embajadores. My husband was asleep with the child in our bed, so I went to sleep on the sofa in the living room so I wouldn't wake them. It was a warm, dark night. An unnatural night, as nights in Madrid are, because Madrid is an unnatural city, situated where no city should be, without natural greenery or water. I remembered something the writer had said, that the most frightening thing about madness is that there isn't an obvious border between wellness and illness. "That's just how it is," he said, "the strange suddenly feels completely normal." I must have been quite well, because right then I couldn't think of anything that felt normal; on the contrary, everything in my life seemed very strange and kind of puckered and illogical. I wished I'd said that to the writer. Maybe he would have said I was fine. But on the other hand – what does it mean when a crazy person tells you you're fine? In my half-drunkenness I couldn't figure it out.

Filomena called at 7 a.m. The sun had started to climb, and the sky over Madrid was light blue and streaked with white contrails. From the window, I could see a few dog owners with their dogs in the park. They spoke in small groups while the dogs ran around and peed, even in the sandboxes, where children, probably including my son, would play in a few hours. Someone dropped out, Filomena said. You can come with us to Granada. It may not be a luxurious trip – it's organized by the city of Madrid – but since you're from France, you might really enjoy getting out and seeing something new. I said I didn't know. My husband only got home yesterday. Well, it's a great opportunity, she added. I woke my husband up and asked him what he thought and he said of course you should go, you have to see Granada. I packed a little bag, showered quickly, and went down to the street. I grabbed a coffee at a bar and then took the metro to Méndez Álvaro, where the bus would be waiting. Everyone from the party was there, fresh, clean, and ready to go. I said hello. The writer was there, too, not looking one bit mad. "*Tu vas bien?*" he said and I answered, "*Mais oui.*" Then we were packed into the coach, and I felt there was something industrial in the way they handled us. The coach was old and brown. "It's like an Almodóvar film," I said. The writer and Filomena looked at me blankly.

The engine started, and the bus began to move. We drove out of Madrid and there was almost no traffic at all. You could sit and look at the houses in peace. Sometimes I did that when we drove around in our car. I would sit and look at the houses, feeling something at the bottom of my stomach, a kind of great terror I was always trying to suppress. Driving on the circular, you could sometimes look right into people's dining rooms and see them sitting around tables and eating, some ten, twenty meters away.

"The most fascinating thing about Madrid," I told the writer, who was sitting next to me, "is the coexistence of so many dimensions. Everything is wall-to-wall: motorways, living rooms, people from South America and people from Europe. We all live with only a few meters or sometimes only decimeters between us. I, for example, have no idea who sleeps on the other side of my bedroom wall."

"It's true," replied the writer. "Everything is curiously put together here. Maybe it feels exotic to someone like you, who comes from elsewhere. But all this coexistence means nothing has a real identity, least of all the city itself."

We sat in silence for a while. Around Aranjuez, Filomena leaned forward and whispered in my ear that she and the writer had made love after I'd left the party.

"Did you?" I said.

"Yes," said Filomena. "And he might look harmless, but in bed he becomes . . . He forces you to do all sorts of things."

She shook her hand in front of her as if she'd burned herself. I laughed at her.

"So, was it good, though?" I said.

"Good for someone like me," she answered, "because I can be both predator and prey at the same time."

Suddenly, I didn't feel like laughing anymore. I blushed without knowing why. The writer stared intently out the window.

There were far too many of us on the coach. I didn't have high expectations, but a little space to put away my bag, stretch my legs, and rest my hands in my lap without poking anyone in the side with my elbow was, I felt, the least you could expect, even if this was a free ride. Yet the bus was crowded, and I couldn't help feeling I was bothering the writer each time I moved, like when I changed the batteries in my camera or ate the tuna baguette I'd bought at the metro. Filomena sat behind us, legs crossed and silent. She ran her hand through her hair from time to time, and I thought she might be upset because I was the one sitting with the writer, not her. I suggested that he change seats, which they both agreed to immediately. The writer sat behind me with Filomena, and then I had two seats to myself. Across the aisle sat a man who was traveling alone. I looked at him and he looked right back at me. He had the curious, pale gaze of the demented. A gaze that seems to see things no one else sees. He smiled at me, and it was an honest and open smile. I smiled back for a while. Then I couldn't keep it up anymore, and I turned away to look out the window again.

"What's your diagnosis?" I heard Filomena ask behind me.

"You know very well there are unwritten rules on trips like these," the writer replied. "You don't talk to each other much, and if you do talk, you never talk about diagnoses or illnesses."

The brown bus continued inland, through the heat. No one said a word; we just looked out the windows at the landscape gliding by. Sand-colored villages rose from the earth like ghost towns. One village seemed as if it were climbing a ledge above a ravine, and at any moment it might lose its fitful grip and fall down. Now and then the guide from Madrid's local authority spoke into the microphone. He had a mildly condescending tone. I soon stopped listening. I closed my eyes and leaned back. I sat like that for a long time. The air-conditioning was on high. It was the only sound, and the hum was monotonous and calming.

"At last, we've arrived in Granada," the guide announced a few hours later.

The bus stopped by the Alhambra, and we got out and stood in a crescent in the car park. A local guide took care of us. He wasn't from Spain either; maybe he was from Morocco. We followed him through the Arabic walkways, listening to the water gurgling in the atria. A hot wind stirred the cypresses, and the stone building radiated a heat that almost burned when you got close.

"Hell must feel like the Arctic compared to this," someone said.

The writer and Filomena held on to each other; they didn't seem to care that they were the only two people I knew on this trip and I was now walking alone. I called my husband at home in Madrid, asked how it was going, and he said don't think about us, make sure to meet people and have fun. It's not that much fun, I said, and he replied that it is what you make of it. We went on through walkways, courtyards, and rooms, and came to some sort of cafeteria, where we drank Arabic tea. Our faces blazed and our tongues burned and the writer said he didn't understand how the Arabs back then could drink such hot tea in this heat.

"Cure ill with ill," the guide said.

We sweated and looked at the walls, which were covered in winding patterns.

"If you're not crazy on arrival, you will be after you've sat a while and looked at these walls," said the writer.

"The untrained eye looks in vain at Moorish art," said the guide. "You Westerners want to see faces and bodies everywhere."

"Is that so?" said the writer.

"Yes, you want to see bodies more than anything," said the guide. "Bodies, bodies, and more bodies."

Silence.

The guide looked at the writer, his gaze lingering as if he were very tired and had forgotten we were even there.

"You can sit there and stare as much as you like," he said eventually. "But the longer you look, the less you'll understand."

He got up and gestured at us, as if to say we should stay. Then he was gone. We hung around for a while, then got up and walked to the parking lot.

*

187

We left Granada and the Alhambra sometime in the afternoon. Once we were on the bus, the driver said the air-conditioning was out of order. Filomena took out her fan, and I fanned myself with a book I had in my bag. Because of the heat, we made an unplanned stop at an insignificant little church. Everyone needed to breathe and, as the guide said, there's nowhere better to breathe than in a church. The church was called Nuestra Señora de la Asunción. We moved toward the entrance. I was last, and I felt dizzy. Filomena and the writer stopped to let me catch up and asked how I was. I said I could still taste the sweetness of the Arabic tea, and I'd left my sunglasses on the coach.

"Take it easy, don't overdo it," they said, going into the church ahead of me.

That was when I saw the mangled angel. At first I didn't understand what was wrong. I stopped and took a few steps back. Above the entrance were five angels. Pompous angels, young boys with fat hands, protruding eyes, and strong jawlines, sculpted from some sort of sandstone. Four had insipid faces, but the fifth angel's features were completely distorted. I looked away. Thought: Surely that angel isn't meant to look like that. I shut my eyes and looked again. But the fifth angel was the same as before: staring out over the landscape as if it had seen something terrible, mouth agape. In spite of the smooth surface, the stone face emanated a feeling of pure horror. The rest of the group had gone inside, and I was alone in the courtyard. He can see something out there, I thought, climbing onto a bench and looking in the same direction as the angel. And there, maybe fifty meters away, I saw the black coat. It took a minute before I understood who it was. My mother-in-law had told me about him once. She said that when you see the angel of death, you know, because he's the only angel dressed all in black. "Spanish superstition," I said at the time. "When he looks at you, your whole body starts to sweat and you start to shake," she said seriously. Then something happens inside of you, something like a twig snapping, and nothing is ever the same again. "Spanish superstition," I repeated, and she replied that of course Northerners know nothing about angels since angels, like so much else, can't live in subzero temperatures.

I shut my eyes. When I opened them again, I saw him clearly. He'd turned to face me, still and black, the earth dead in the background. The hot wind stirred his coat and he stared at me, eyes flaming.

I must have fainted, because when I opened my eyes again, I was lying inside the church and Filomena was fanning my face. The writer was next to her, looking at me with anticipation, and the guide was stroking water on my cheeks. I remembered the angel instantly.

"I saw something out there," I said and stood up. "Someone standing in a black coat in the distance."

"Ah – the priest," said the writer, avoiding eye contact.

"Don't you start now," the guide said.

"Start what?" I asked.

"Don't play dumb," he said. "Just go out and sit on the bus."

Back in the courtyard, the five swollen angels now looked identical. The fifth looked exactly like the other four – dense and even, staring indifferently ahead. I climbed onto the bench and looked out over the landscape. Black and yellow spots danced in my field of vision, as sometimes happens in the heat.

"I had a Sicilian lover once," said Filomena when we were sitting on the coach again.

"Oh?" said the writer.

"Yes, I did," she said, as if she doubted he believed her. "It's true."

"I believe you," he said.

"What's your diagnosis?" she asked again. And when he didn't answer:

"It's anxiety-related, right? It's in your face. It looks broken."

"Don't be so hard on my face," the writer said. "If you'd been through what I've been through, you'd be happy to have a face at all."

Filomena scoffed. We drove through a village with aluminum-framed windows and elderly people dressed in black sitting outside the buildings.

When we got back to Madrid, it was late. The day's heat radiated from the sidewalk. We said our goodbyes, suddenly polite and stiff. Maybe we were just tired. I wanted to talk to the writer about madness and normality, a quick word, to see if he, too, knew my mother-in-law's story about the angel of death, and what he thought the guide had meant when he told me not to start. And the angel on the church – seeing things in the heat doesn't mean you're crazy, right? I thought: I'll just ask the writer if he wants to go for a drink. But the writer didn't seem to be in the mood; he was stroking his stubble, and he looked worried. Never mind, I thought. Anyway, I'm not afraid of going mad, I'm more afraid that everything will go to hell.

Everyone else went home. I wanted to do the same, but going home like this – carrying with me the feeling of a scorched hinterland, visions, all these thoughts of madness – felt wrong. It would be like walking into a clean apartment in dirty shoes, I thought. So instead of taking the metro to Legazpi, I took it to Goya and walked toward Retiro. There was a long line outside the Renoir cinema. I joined it and bought a ticket. (I asked for any ticket they had, and the woman in the window gave me one from the tallest stack in front of her.) I went into the cinema and sat down. It was painted red and had black chairs and small round lamps screwed into the walls. A few rows behind me sat two older women. They spoke in hoarse voices about immigrants. One said the Dominican ones were responsible for 95 percent of the crime in her neighborhood, and then the other asked if she'd seen any statistics and the first one replied that you didn't need to, you could tell that was how things were just by living there.

The film began. Sean Penn was wandering around a large house. He had teased black hair and was made up like an old lady or a singer in a rock band. For the rest of the movie, he dragged around a wheelie suitcase. The director – Sean Penn himself, apparently – seemed to be imitating aspects of Tarantino's style, but whereas Tarantino knows what he's doing, Sean Penn didn't seem to have a clue. The ladies behind me snored loudly. I thought about the trip. I thought about the writer and Filomena and wondered what exactly he had forced her to do. I tried to picture the writer forcing Filomena into something, but it was impossible. Maybe they were lying. Maybe they'd been teasing me. And in what way was she both prey and predator? I couldn't picture that either. Then I considered telling my husband about the angel of death. He's a rational person, but he has a deep Spanish vein that makes him superstitious. When you hit that vein there's no limit to what he'll believe. I was afraid something would happen to our son and that the angel of death was an omen, so

I decided not to mention it to my husband because shared fear, just like shared happiness, is doubled. I wondered what to have for dinner the next night and remembered I had a can of tuna in the pantry, but then I remembered that my husband was home and we should make sure to have a good meal. That big, flat fish called mahi-mahi. Or bass. Or steamed black Galician mussels. Then I thought what difference did it make; nothing really mattered.

Back on the street again, white clouds crowded the dark sky. They galloped by and the wind blew through the streets. My cell phone rang and I answered. It was Filomena.

"I saw the angel of death, too," she said.

"What?" I said.

"I saw him too. And so did the writer, and Juan, the guy who insisted on staying on the bus."

I remembered his pale, demented look.

"Why didn't you say?" I said.

"I'm afraid, too."

"Of what?'"

"Of everything falling apart."

"Exactly what might fall apart, Filomena?"

The line rustled, and I thought she'd hang up. But the rustling stopped, and I heard her voice clearly.

"I don't know. The face, maybe. Or the face and the body. Or the face, the body, and your whole life. Everything."

I didn't know what to say.

"Maybe we'll talk again sometime," I said after a while.

"I don't think so," she said.

We hung up. Down in the metro I passed a man with dreadlocks holding out a paper cup. I didn't put anything in it, but when I walked by I heard him whisper: *Don't give up baby, keep on struggle baby, everything will be fine baby.*

THE YEAR OF THE PIG

I suppose none of this would have happened if not for a dream I had when I was young, in which a woman told me I would at some point guide someone through the apocalypse. Talking about this dream embarrasses me. But I'm even more embarrassed by the influence it has had on me over the years. The thing is, it comes to mind when I get drunk. As sure as a cork in water, it rises to the surface the second I loosen my grip. Sometimes it makes me feel chosen, and I start scanning the faces of the people around me. Who am I supposed to guide, how will I do it, and, above all: when can I expect the apocalypse?

It was the end of January in Madrid, and I'd been invited to a party in Chinatown. Don't let people tell you the Chinese aren't drinkers. This was a New Year's party, and everyone was soaking up the alcohol like a sponge – it wasn't just rice wine and *baijiu*, either. There was anything and everything. Whiskey, wine, and beer gushed down their throats, and mine too, for that matter. While I was still sober, I was told the Chinese New Year is different to New Year's in the West, in part because it comes a few weeks later, and in part because the celebration lasts more than just a few hours of build-up to an "orgasmic" (the word was spoken with contempt) crescendo of champagne and fireworks, followed by a daylong, nationwide hangover. The Chinese New Year, I was told, spanned days, sometimes weeks. This was a period of time that expanded toward its breaking point, where it would sort of dissolve, only to take shape as something new. On top of all that, with the passing of each year you got one year older. An animal, too, could transform into another. We were about to go from the Year of the Dog to the Year of the Pig. This business about being turned from a dog into a pig hardly sounded encouraging to me, but then I was told it was about seeing the positive traits in the animals and taking a positive view – a pig was not dirty and lusty, but generous, empathic, and loyal.

Anyway. All I can say is we partied. We were rowdy and we drank, and in our careening and carousing we were birds of a feather, no matter if we came from China or northern Europe. The party went on for so long I could only tell the days were passing by the way the light filtered through the blinds in the guest bedroom. From a warm yellow flicker at night, to cold and harsh in the daytime. Because of the sustained drunkenness, I can only recall fragments of the conversations around me. I remember hearing the host explaining to someone that I was from Sweden, and women in Sweden make sure to give men a hard time. I also seem to remember some of them studying my hand at some point, searching for signs of frostbite. I was drifting in and out of sleep all that time, and the apocalypse dream plagued me more than ever. I writhed in my own sweat, wondering who I was going to save and when. Even when I finally emerged from the fog, I felt hot and feverish, and I was obsessed with a brand-new thought: Do good. It's not that I thought I'd been bad in my previous life, more that (and this applies not just to me but to most of humanity) I'd been wrapped up in a kind of narcissism that had never sat right, but which I'd never managed to shift. But now, awake and facing the year's end, I felt all that weight and darkness leaving me, like a tumor that had finally dried out and was about to fall off. In this overheated state of transformation, which happened on the tenth day, I started drifting around Chinatown. Out on the sidewalk, I suddenly realized I wasn't wearing the same clothes I'd had on when I'd arrived at the party. I think I'd been wearing black, because I always wear black when I feel insecure. Now, I was wearing mint-green tights and a pink blazer over a pale yellow dress that fluttered around my calves and hardly seemed suitable for someone my age. The unlikeliness of my outfit seemed to make other unlikely things possible. I actually think the pale yellow dress was the reason I came up with the idea of performing a miracle at all. And the more I thought about it, and the more I sipped from the bottle I'd taken from my hosts' bar and stowed in my bag, the more I felt that a single paltry miracle was insufficient, somehow. I thought about my dream. I thought about how people do in fact always have a choice: stick with the old, or try something new.

I went back to my hosts' apartment, which was on the lower ground floor of a ramshackle three-story building, and on the back of a piece of cardboard I'd found in the trash, I wrote: *Hacedora de milagros* (that is: *Miracle Worker*). I wasn't entirely sure if the Spanish was correct, but I assumed whoever read it wouldn't exactly know either, because it was mostly Chinese people who lived in the area and the Chinese don't really care about Spanish. I fixed the sign to the door, and then I sat down and waited. My plan was simple. I would try to perform a miracle by holding people's hands in mine, closing my eyes, and hoping. If there was any truth at all in the apocalypse dream, then things would start to manifest. After a few hours, my first client arrived. It was a woman who suffered from terrible insomnia. I asked her to sit on the floor. She did. I sat in front of her and gripped her hands. We sat like that for several minutes and nothing happened. Finally, the woman began to fidget and said it was probably time for her to go home and make lunch for her husband. Then something struck me, and I asked her to take off her shirt. First, she gave me a hostile look, but then she complied. With her sitting there topless, her hands covering her breasts, I took off my shirt, too. I crouched down behind her and embraced her. My bare skin was pressing against her bare back. I closed my eyes and tried to imagine my hand making its way inside her body, past layers of fat, muscle, and ribs, and finally taking hold of her heart. I took great pains to ensure I held it with care, as though the heart were a fragile bird being offered the chance to feel at peace in my hand. All the while, I did my utmost to picture the woman in a deep, tranquil slumber. Then we sat like that. I don't know how long we were there, but it was a long time. The woman's breathing became calmer, maybe she even nodded off. I got up and said she could go home now, and she'd be able to sleep. She got up and left. I stood in the window and watched her go. The emptiness I felt inside was indescribable.

The woman came back the next day. Her face was so open and smooth compared to the day before, and she told me she'd slept for fifteen hours straight. Her eyes were sparkling with joy, and she took my hand and kissed it several times, as though I were in fact a miracle worker. Then she went out and told all of her female friends, who in turn told theirs, and then they told their families and acquaintances. I was fully booked for several days. And I always did the same thing. Skin to skin, their hearts in my hand, my hand warming them. It was all I needed to do, and then the miracle seemed to happen on its own.

On the last day of the Chinese New Year, the businessman Lee Peng arrived. His appearance wasn't in any way remarkable, and yet I noticed him long before he reached my door. A small man, wearing fake leather shoes and too-big brown pants made of a synthetic fabric, cinched tight at the waist with a belt. He walked fast, and with each step his grimy hems dragged across the cobbles. When he approached me, I saw that his clothes were dirty but he was well put together, as though he knew how to be proper and wanted to be, but didn't have access to a washing machine.

"You're my last hope," he said.

"Go on, Mr. Peng," I said.

He sat there for a while, quietly. The only sound that broke the silence was the traffic on Gran Vía and the upstairs neighbor listening to a breakfast show on Channel Five. Finally, he started to speak. He told me he'd done everything in his life wrong. He'd been unfaithful to his wife, and unfaithful to everyone he'd cheated on her with, because he never told them he was married. "My flesh," he said. "It's my flesh. It has destroyed me and everything around me." But the worst part was his children, how his behavior had cast a shadow over them, too. Now they hated him. Everybody hated him. The betrayed ex-wife, his angry lovers, his children. One evening, he had an idea. Even if he hadn't been a good role model in life, he wanted to leave the stage with his head held high. This was how he saw his salvation: leaving the stage, his head held high. It would be said that he'd lived his life like a dog, but in death he'd become a man. "Or a pig," I said, but by the look he gave me I don't think he understood.

"This is why I decided to explore the possibility of selling my organs. I read an article about a village in Pakistan where almost every villager had only one kidney, because they'd sold the other one to the rich people who traveled there for new kidneys. *There is an industry*, it said. *Flesh generates activity around itself like few other things. If you're looking, there's always a meat market to be found, for we live in an age of flesh.*"

Indeed: on the black market Lee Peng had sought and found his buyer.

"The black market is a brave new world," he said. "A world of possibility for the desperate, a gulp of seawater for the shipwrecked. In the land of the blind, the one-eyed man is king, they say. You go from being nobody to being somebody who has everything. I had been a living failure, and now I was a 'Source of Life.' That's what they call us."

Lee Peng had sold both of his kidneys, his liver, and his heart. For this, he'd been promised 10,000 euros, money that would be sent to his children as soon as the operation was done. The operation would take place one night at a large hotel outside of Madrid, where the Sources of Life would meet their recipients together with a team of surgeons. The Sources of Life would then have various substances injected into them, substances that would help them enjoy their final night. They would eat a wonderful dinner in wonderful company. No, in his moment of death Lee Peng would not even want for a woman. Lee Peng thought this was the answer to all of his problems. He would have a painless death, perhaps even a happy death, and his children would receive an inheritance.

"It doesn't get better than that for a person like me," he said.

But the closer he got to the operation, the colder Lee Peng's feet became. Now there were only two days to go, and for the past day Lee Peng had felt he no longer wanted to die. He'd been sitting in the sun, watching the people go by in Chinatown. He'd looked out over the crowds, the young and the old, the animals and the traffic. And somewhere in all that, he'd realized everything was defective, not just him. He may have done the wrong things, but when it came down to it, he was no worse than anyone else, and he could still strive to set things right. He would work, and be there for his children and his ex-wife. He had a long to-do list, but when he called the man who was handling the organ exchange, he was told it was too late.

"You can't back out now, Mr. Peng," the man said. "Your organs have already been sold, and a powerful man is going to be given your heart. The fact of the matter is, he already considers it his."

When he finished telling me this, Lee Peng's forehead was drenched in sweat. I asked him what he wanted me to do, because this seemed to fall far outside of what could be considered my area of expertise. He said he wanted to feel at peace, at a great and incredible peace. The peace would aid him, whatever was at his door. I said I'd do what I could and asked him to take off his shirt. Lee Peng did as I said, and I took off mine as usual. I crouched down and embraced him. The room was cold, so I got up and fetched a blanket and swept it around us both. We sat like that. After a while, Lee Peng began to cry. He cried like I'd never heard anyone cry before. He blubbered, the snot ran, he whimpered and whined. I think he was crying for a full half hour. Then he wiped his face and nose with one corner of the blanket and collapsed in my arms, like a sack of hot soil. I kept holding him, and was just about to visualize my hand slowly but surely finding its way inside, gently taking hold of his heart and warming it, when I became aware of something peculiar. Before I could picture my own hand, I felt another hand slowly searching inside me. I sat as still as a stone pillar. All the while Lee Peng's hand was finding its way through my flesh, past my ribs, toward my heart, where he carefully took hold of me. The affection I felt in that moment was overwhelming. I cried so hard I was almost screaming. But Lee Peng kept holding me, until all the tears were out and, exhausted, I fell to the floor. Then he let go and got up. He stood there in the middle of the room, in those brown pants with that belt. He said:

"Thank you."

And then he was gone.

For several days, I waited for Lee Peng to return. During that time I couldn't perform any miracles, so I took down the sign and told everyone that the time for miracles was done. An old woman nodded and said, yes, everything was in its place, one year had become another, what had dissolved had found a new form. After a few days, I took off the pale yellow dress and put on my black clothes again. Then I left Chinatown and took the metro to Ventas, where I had a room.

What happened to Lee Peng? I'm not entirely sure, but a few weeks after our encounter I was standing at the bus stop by Diego de León when I became aware of something strange. It started with a pain under my shoulder blade and was followed by the intense sensation of something hot and utterly human finding its way inside me. The pain stopped, and I felt a featherlight touch near my heart.

The only other time I'd experienced anything like it was with Lee Peng. I turned around and searched the crowded sidewalk, but I couldn't find his face. I looked out into the street, into the traffic, and my gaze landed on a black car being escorted by a motorcade of other black cars. One of the windows was rolled down, and a man was looking right at me. "Lee Peng!" I called out to him. "Is that you?" But it wasn't Lee Peng, because Lee Peng had a different skin color and a different face. When the man heard me shouting, his face filled with fright. The window rolled up, and the car disappeared down Avenida de América.

Dear readers,

As well as relying on bookshop sales, And Other Stories relies on subscriptions from people like you for many of our books, whose stories other publishers often consider too risky to take on.

Our subscribers don't just make the books physically happen. They also help us approach booksellers, because we can demonstrate that our books already have readers and fans. And they give us the security to publish in line with our values, which are collaborative, imaginative and 'shamelessly literary'.

All of our subscribers:

- receive a first-edition copy of each of the books they subscribe to
- are thanked by name at the end of our subscriber-supported books
- receive little extras from us by way of thank you, for example: postcards created by our authors

BECOME A SUBSCRIBER,
OR GIVE A SUBSCRIPTION TO A FRIEND

Visit andotherstories.org/subscriptions to help make our books happen. You can subscribe to books we're in the process of making. To purchase books we have already published, we urge you to support your local or favourite bookshop and order directly from them – the often unsung heroes of publishing.

OTHER WAYS TO GET INVOLVED

If you'd like to know about upcoming events and reading groups (our foreign-language reading groups help us choose books to publish, for example) you can:

- join our mailing list at: andotherstories.org
- follow us on Twitter: @andothertweets
- join us on Facebook: facebook.com/AndOtherStoriesBooks
- admire our books on Instagram: @andotherpics
- follow our blog: andotherstories.org/ampersand

CURRENT & UPCOMING BOOKS

Swedish writer LINA WOLFF has lived and worked in Italy and Spain. During her years in Valencia and Madrid, she began to write her short-story collection *Many People Die Like You. Bret Easton Ellis and the Other Dogs*, her first novel, was awarded the prestigious *Vi* Magazine Literature Prize and shortlisted for the prestigious 2013 Swedish Radio Award for Best Novel of the Year. It was published by And Other Stories in 2016, followed by her second novel, *The Polyglot Lovers*, in 2019. Wolff now lives in southern Sweden.

SASKIA VOGEL is an author and translator from Los Angeles, now living in Berlin. *Permission*, her debut novel, was published in English, Spanish, French and Swedish in 2019. She has translated leading Swedish authors such as Karolina Ramqvist, Katrine Marcal, and Lena Andersson. Her translations and writing have appeared in publications such as *Granta*, *Guernica*, *The White Review*, *The Offing*, *Paris Review Daily* and *The Quietus*. Her translation of Lina Wolff's *The Polyglot Lovers* was awarded the English PEN Translates award.